SILVER SERIES

SUPERB WRITING
TO FIRE THE IMAGINATION

W.J. Corbett writes: 'The clans of the People were living orderly lives on the earth when humans appeared. But size was might and the People soon had cause to hide from the fierce giants. Sometimes by chance the humans and the People met and legends were born and spread through mutual fear and suspicion.

So began the age old enmity and fear between the large and the small. Dark tales of mischievous magic were whispered around the firesides of the humans. In turn the People taught their young ones to flee the giants who trampled and destroyed with thoughtless brutality. And so for countless generations the People and the humans lived uneasily together, each avoiding the other.

The *Ark of the People* sequence contains stories of the Willow Clan taken from their history books – their loves and laughter and their courageous battles.'

Born in Warwickshire, W.J. Corbett joined the Merchant Navy as a galley-boy when he was sixteen and saw the world. His first book, *The Song of Pentecost*, won the prestigious Whitbread Award.

'Mr Corbett has wit, originality and economy with words which put him straight in the very top class of all . . . beside the authors of such classics as *The Wind in the Willows.*' Auberon Waugh, *Daily Mail*

By W.J. Corbett,
published by Hodder Children's Books:

THE ARK OF THE PEOPLE SEQUENCE
The Ark of the People
The Quest for the End of the Tail
The Spell to Save the Golden Snake
ALSO:
The Dragon's Egg and Other Stories
The Battle of Chinnbrook Wood

Other Silver titles:

Lord of the Dance
Judy Allen

The Osmid Version
Nell Coleman

Marco's Millions
Interstellar Pig
William Sleator

The Castle of Dark
East of Midnight
Tanith Lee

THE QUEST FOR THE END OF THE TAIL

W·J·CORBETT

Illustrated by Wayne Anderson

Hodder
Children's
Books

A division of Hodder Headline Limited

Text copyright © 2000 W.J. Corbett
Illustrations copyright © 2000 Wayne Anderson

First published in Great Britain in 2000
by Hodder Children's Books

This edition published in 2002

A Catalogue record for this book
is available from the British Library

ISBN 0 340 77340 5

Typeset by Hewer Text Ltd, Edinburgh
Printed and bound in Great Britain by
Clays Ltd, St Ives plc

Hodder Children's Books
A Division of Hodder Headline Limited
338 Euston Road
London NW1 3BH

Contents

One

THE CAVE OF TEARS

And it came to pass that the People and their friends aboard the ark were safely delivered from their destroyed valley by the waters of the River of Dreams. Flowing through time and space, the tides had drifted them back through the centuries to their old valley as it had been before the humans had arrived to flood it with their reservoir. Now the Willow clan and their friends could rejoice in the paradise the waters had guided them to. They were soon exploring their long-ago valley with a freedom from fear they had never known. It was bliss to stroll over the hills and relax beside the swift stream which raced between the willow and oak trees that graced its banks. Yet though the human danger no longer existed, the Willow clan could not ignore a yearning deep inside them.

The Willow clan of the valley had always made their homes in the branches of oak trees. Their histories read it, their instincts urged it. And so after the thrill of exploring their surroundings they set to and began to build their new homes high above the earth. The carpenters were soon busy chopping and sawing and hammering inside the huge limbs of the oak to create the winding passages, the meeting halls and the sleeping quarters necessary for a comfortable life. Very important was Granny Willow's kitchen where she could bake acorn bread and create the delicious herb and vegetable stews for which she was famous. The library in a quiet corner of a bough was also fashioned with care. It would house the histories and the poetry of the People where the young could learn and study.

Just when the library was completed it was unfortunate that a fierce argument erupted about the stacking of the books on the shelves. Two small poets stood shouting and glaring at each other in that sacred place. They caused such a commotion that Robin and Fern, the leaders of the Willow clan, were hastily called to intervene.

'That's quite enough from you two,' said Robin, parting them. 'Why all this fuss, what's the problem?'

'Teasel's the problem,' wept Meadowsweet. 'I'd just stacked my favourite poetry books on the shelf that catches the light when Teasel came swaggering in. He sneered and swept my books to the floor saying they were rubbish. Then he stacked his own favourite books in their place.

Just look at the blasphemy Teasel has wantonly committed. See how some of our greatest poets are lying on their spines with their pages fluttering in the draught. How can he be so arrogant and cruel? Robin, Fern, I beg that you make an example of him. He deserves to be punished for doing such a wicked thing.'

'What do you say, Teasel?' said Robin sternly, turning to face the bristling boy. 'I hope you've got a humble apology ready.'

'Meadowsweet came poking her nose in,' said Teasel defiantly. 'I was managing the library perfectly well on my own until she came flouncing in. She knows nothing about stacking books in order of merit. If she had her way all the shelves would be crammed with books about butterflies and primroses and all that silly mush. The real, gritty poems of our clan mean nothing to her scatty mind!'

'That's unfair!' snapped Fern. 'Everyone in our Willow clan is entitled to their opinions about things. Now, you'll apologise to

Meadowsweet and pick up the books you've shamefully scattered on the floor.'

'Then together you'll agree to share the shelf in the light with all kinds of books,' ordered Robin.

'Won't!' shouted Teasel.

'Yes you will!' cried Meadowsweet.

Then they were interrupted. The magpie had poked his beak and one beady eye through a knothole in the library wall.

'Robin,' he croaked. 'You and Fern must come at once. The young ones have made an astonishing discovery on the hill above our tree.'

'Are they in danger?' said Robin, alarmed. 'What kind of discovery?'

'Not more trouble,' murmured Fern, pressing her palms to her cheeks.

'You'd best come and see for yourselves,' advised the excited bird. 'As your official scout I can only guide you to a certain buttercup patch on the hill. It's for you to sort out what's gone badly wrong for those out-of-control small ones.'

The bitter argument about books and dead poets was forgotten as Robin and Fern hurried away to investigate. They were closely followed by Meadowsweet and Teasel who were as curious as anyone to witness astonishing discoveries made in buttercup patches. Meanwhile the pages of the books strewn on the floor continued to flutter in the spring breeze that sighed in through the knothole in that hallowed place which was quiet once again.

It seemed that while the young ones had been exploring the hill, Coltsfoot had suddenly vanished from the face of the earth. He had never disappeared before which made this first time very strange. His close friend Foxglove, though distressed, was firm in her mind. Coltsfoot would never vanish to anywhere without telling her first. Which made it more puzzling. Then someone suggested they should examine the exact spot where Coltsfoot had last been seen. It was agreed that at the last sighting he had been barging through the buttercup stems towards the centre of the clump. He had obviously lost his way among the forest of green stalks. An urgent search was mounted, his anxious friends forming a large circle and then advancing through the buttercup patch towards its centre. Meeting in the middle with not one glimpse of Coltsfoot they were as stumped as ever. Which made the situation not only curious but alarming. For the navigating skills of Coltsfoot were legendary. Hadn't he in company with Foxglove and Finn of the Fisher clan expertly steered the ark during the perilous journey to reach this re-born valley? How could a boy with such a keen sense of direction lose his way inside a mere clump of buttercups? His tired friends pondered this puzzle as they slumped down in the middle of the patch, many wearing bright yellow caps donated by the shaken buttercups. It was in a mood of near-mourning when an alert youngster shouted that he could hear a voice echoing up from below their feet. Everyone craned their ears. He was right. Then someone cried out and pointed to a strange hole in the ground. It became larger as everyone jumped to their feet to crowd and stomp around its crumbling edges. Then it came again, a faint voice from below.

'Hello!' they yelled down. 'Is that you, Coltsfoot? If it is shout "yes", if it isn't shout "no".'

'Of course I'm Coltsfoot,' came the impatient reply. 'But be quiet for I have some astounding news. If you could see what I'm gazing at you'd be stunned with shock and wonder.'

'We're stunned already, Coltsfoot,' scolded Foxglove down the hole. 'Stunned that you should worry us to death by getting lost for a prank. If you don't climb back up at once we're going to tell Robin and Fern about your silly joke. How dare you hide down holes when we're all sick with worry up top.'

'I'm not hiding, I fell down here,' shouted Coltsfoot. 'And I'm in a strange cave with a huge golden snake weeping tears all over me.

Why don't you fall down the hole and join me? But be warned, if you have tears be prepared to shed them now, for I haven't stopped crying since I arrived here.'

'Stop romancing and pull yourself together,' said Foxglove sharply. 'We've worn ourselves out searching for you. Come up into the fresh air and get some sense back into your head – oh-oh . . . what's happening?'

The crumbling ground suddenly collapsed even more, sending the screaming youngsters plummeting down into the cave. Their wish to be reunited with Coltsfoot had been swiftly granted. The ever-nosy magpie who had been watching and listening above was filled with alarm to see the small ones tumbling into the hole. This was what sent him skimming back to the oak in a flurry of feathers and wings. This was why Robin and Fern and the others were crashing through the buttercups guided by the anxious bird. Arriving, they gazed fearfully down into the now, very large hole in the middle of the buttercup patch. To their bewilderment a pale, golden glow met their eyes. A glow so misty that they could make out little else.

'Are there any broken bones down there?' called worried Fern. 'Just hang on, we'll be down to rescue you as soon as we can.'

'Only our hearts are broken,' came the sad reply. 'For we're gazing into the saddest green eyes in the world. And we're listening to a story that would break the stoniest heart. So we've decided to stay down here with the Great Golden Snake and his kind guardians and help to ease the suffering he's endured since time began.'

'You'll be rescued and like it,' snapped Robin. 'You can play games of imagination just as well above ground. We're going to weave a rope and climb down. So let's have no more of your nonsense.'

A rope was quickly made from woven grasses. Securing one end to a strong buttercup stalk, Robin and Fern and the others swarmed down into the strangely glowing cave. Their wildest dreams could not have conjured the eerie scene they saw. The huge cave was almost taken up by the head of a gigantic golden snake. Its emerald-green eyes glowed in the semi-light and dripped a steady rain of lemon tears into the pool beneath its nose. A long forked tongue flicked to and fro between thin embittered lips as the great snake murmured and sighed in a piteous way. Though angry, Robin and Fern felt their own eyes brimming with tears to see such distress. The young ones who had been in the cave longer were weeping and wailing like veterans, their heads buried in their hands as they shared the grief of the snake they had barely met. Throughout all this a small group of strangers were bustling about tending the snake and quite ignoring the crowd of gawkers who had dropped in on them. They were dressed in a curious fashion. They wore tight-fitting suits and caps of a dull yellow colour. Their skin was ivory-pale and their hands bony and wrinkled as if from too much immersion in water. Yet it was clear from their size and their snub noses that they were of the People, though what kind of People? And why did they tend the great snake so lovingly? Robin waded into the pool of golden tears and spoke to one of the workers who was busily scrubbing the huge nose of their charge. Robin was relieved to be greeted not with a frown but a cheerful grin.

'Excuse me,' said the Willow leader politely. 'I'm Robin of the Willow clan and we live above the ground in an oak tree.'

'I'm very pleased for you,' smiled the worker, pausing in mid-scrub. 'I'm Umber of the Guardian clan and I'm also very pleased for myself. It's nice to be pleased in this world of sadness, don't you think?'

'I apologise for us dropping into your cave uninvited,' said Robin, still very much confused. 'I'm sorry if the lives of you and your great snake have been disrupted, but the earth above just opened up and some of us fell down.'

'No worries,' grinned Umber. 'We're pleased to see you. It's very rare we have visitors from other People. We only wish they'd drop in more often to brighten up our lonely lives of total dedication to our Great Snake. We adore to smile and dance whenever we get the chance.'

'And we're pleased to meet you too,' said Robin. 'But may I be bold and ask why you and your Guardian friends scrub and polish the Great Snake's head in such a dedicated way?'

'To keep him happy and beautiful, of course,' said Umber. 'Our clan histories are clear on that point. So long as his head is in our charge it's our duty to tend it. But I explained this earlier to the little visitor who dropped in first.'

'Which was me!' shouted Coltsfoot, annoyed. 'Folk should remember that I'm the explorer who discovered this cave. I say this just in case Robin tries to claim the credit and the glory as leaders usually do.'

'Another word from you and you can climb the rope and report home,' warned Robin. 'Just speak when you're spoken to, impudent scamp.'

'I'd like to know where the rest of the snake is,' interrupted Fern. 'We can see his huge trapped head clearly enough, but where's the rest of his body?'

'That is his sadness, and the sadness of us all,' sighed Umber. 'Our histories say that while his head has been trapped here since birth, the rest of him winds around the hills and valleys of the land of the People. We in this cave of tears tend his head and also his neck which extends into the cavern beyond; we're expected to do no more. Other groups of our Guardian clan look after his far-flung portions. We in this cave can only do what our histories bid us, and that we happily do.'

'So the Great Golden Snake is divided from himself?' said Fern, pityingly. 'I'd like to hear his whole story if you can bear to tell it.'

'It's a tale that will make you cry,' warned Umber. 'But if you really want to know then here goes . . .'

14

And so with Robin and Fern and the youngsters listening raptly, Umber launched into the history of the Great Golden Snake.

'Our snake was born one thousand years ago, give or take,' began Umber. 'But he was a Great Golden Snake with a difference. For still only days old he began to freakishly outgrow his family. While they had tails to admire and curl up with at night his own was fast vanishing from this home cave as he grew and grew. As his family died and the centuries passed his body was winding and coiling through the forests and plains, over the rivers and the mountains of our world of the People, his head stuck fast in this cave. He tried to sleep the time away but couldn't. Never once in his one thousand years of life has he closed his eyes and slept. It was impossible. For as every snake on earth knows, without the end of one's tail to curl up with, sleep will never come. We of the People can hug ourselves for comfort and drift off into our dreams. But our great snake has nothing to hug but the bitter memory of his vanished tail that has kept him awake every night and day of his long life. That is why the Great Golden Snake weeps constantly into the pool of his tears. Every beat of his heart is a second nearer to dying alone without his tail for comfort.'

'I'd have died of loneliness ages ago,' wept Meadowsweet. 'I'd even welcome Teasel as company after one thousand years of being alone.'

'I'll try to work out that compliment, if it is one,' grinned Teasel.

'Shush,' said Fern, annoyed. 'Do go on, Umber.'

'Sometimes his loneliness became too much to bear,' went on Umber. 'He often felt like ending it all by starving himself to death, denying himself the tasty, silver fishes darting through his pool of tears. But his sanity was saved. For by swivelling his green eyes upwards he could see the stars shining in through the peephole above his head. They became the companions of his isolation. They became his friends, silently listening as he raged about the dreary sameness of his too-long life. It was as if they sympathised, they also knowing the agony of an eternity that never seemed to end. He had no notion that his misery afforded others great delight.'

'What others?' said Robin, puzzled.

Umber continued. 'As the ages passed, his growing and twisting body became a fixed land-mark for the herds of deer galloping along his midriff for their rich spring grazing lands. Birds and small animals came to build their homes in the security of the tangled creepers and bushes that draped his enormous sides. Soon the great snake became as enduring and as familiar as the landscape he coiled around. His body was a world in itself for the creatures who huddled close to his protection as the fierce ones stalked the night. They knew nothing of the anguished heart of the host who gave them shelter. They were simply grateful for him being there with no thought that he might need comfort too.'

'Where do you Guardians come in?' asked Foxglove, fascinated.

'It was later during the snake's tortured life when the People appeared in these valleys and forests they would make their own,' smiled Umber. 'All of our clans have our histories of those times. It is written that a wandering group of the People discovered this cave and the great snake's trapped head. They were moved to pity as he sobbed out his tragic life story. From that moment those people became our clan of Guardians, vowing that they would tend his needs and never desert him no matter what. Soon our clan became strung out along the Great Snake's bulk, brushing and scrubbing when he shed his old skin to help him look spry and young. We in this cave made sure of his supplies of fish and also his favourite snacks of wild honey. But sadly, we Guardians could not bring his tail safe home and grant him the sleep he craved. We just did our best for our giant friend which was all that we could do.

And that is the story up to the present day,' ended Umber, sighing deeply.

'Oh, you poor dear snake,' cried Meadow-sweet, splashing through the tears to pat the tip of the giant's nose. 'How sadly romantic your history is.'

'If only we could help,' said Robin, deeply moved. 'Have you any idea where the tail could be at this point in its wanderings? Perhaps it's well on the way home to the cave. After hundreds of years of travel it must yearn to be reunited with its head. After all, every journey must end no matter how twisting and turning the road might be. And it must be very boring snaking through forests and squirming up mountains when one is blind and journeying backwards, as it were. But that poses a problem. Can a tail have a mind of its own?'

'Can a tail yearn to return to its roots?' nodded Fern. 'That's certainly a puzzling problem.'

'Of course not!' shouted Coltsfoot. 'My head

is yearning to go home after all this clap-trap talk, yet my big toe is quite unmoved. That's because it can't think, and neither can a tail however well travelled.'

'I won't warn you again,' said Robin, wagging his finger.

'We just don't know where the tail might be,' said Umber, shrugging helplessly. 'We can only look after the head and the neck of our snake.'

'I know what more could be done!' yelled Coltsfoot. 'I defy Robin's final warning to shut up. I insist that an expedition is launched at once to track down the end of this runaway tail. The stubborn tip must be forced to return to its snivelling head as soon as possible. Only then will all this weeping and wailing stop. I propose that a scientific expedition is organised at once to travel the length of the Great Snake, to find out what's holding the tail up in its coming home. The quest must be equipped with hard rations and bristling weapons in case it meets with hardship and foul play along the way. And

I know just the person to lead the expedition. No other than Finn of the Fisher clan who's an expert explorer and my idol. With his knowledge of the heavens and the stars he'll pinpoint the precise position of that stubborn tail and send it packing back to this cave where it belongs. Then afterwards the members of the quest will stride home to the oak in the valley, bloody and triumphant and hailed as heroes.'

'As leader of the Willow clan I'll decide about an expedition and who'll lead it,' said Robin, seething.

'I agree you've been a great past leader, Robin,' said Coltsfoot. 'But you aren't as young as you were, and you know nothing about navigating by the stars. Now Finn is much younger than you and he carries a map of the stars in his head. Only yesterday he told me about a Black Hole in space he'd just discovered. He intends to explore it one day when he's learned how to fly. With respect, Robin, what do you know about Black Holes in space?'

'I know about one black hole,' said angry Robin, pointing. 'And there's a rope dangling down from it. I'm ordering you to climb it and hurry back to our oak to help Granny Willow with the washing-up. Off you go, and don't argue.'

Deeply shamed, Coltsfoot slouched across to the rope and silently shinned up it. His close friend Foxglove looked distressed as his small figure stood outlined against the afternoon sun before turning for home, his head hanging. For long moments her loyalties were torn as she considered climbing the rope after Coltsfoot in protest. But respect won out. Robin was her leader after all. She stayed to listen to the many opinions being voiced in this strange cave of tears.

'Could I ask you, Umber?' said Fern, puzzled. 'Have you Guardians never thought about sending an expedition to the end of your Great Snake's tail? You say your clan is strung out along his length. Haven't you thought of getting together and sorting the problem out?'

'I can only speak for the Guardians in this cave,' said Umber. 'We have no contact with the members of our clan who tend him above ground. And your question is hurtful, Fern. Catering to the needs of our great snake is a full-time job.'

Another Guardian spoke, her tone indignant. 'Who do you think panders to his every whim? Who do you think keeps him supplied with the silver fishes and the mushrooms, and the delicious honeycombs he adores and craves? And who do you think have to brave the stings of angry bees to provide him with his luxuries?'

'Not to mention having to mop his swollen and weeping eyes all the time,' cried another Guardian, balanced on the nose of their great charge. He waved a clump of sodden moss in anger. 'This is my life, and it takes up every second of it. Do I complain? I have no time to complain while the tears of our friend keep ever-flowing. I've no time to consider hunting down tails with this head to look after.'

'In other words you Guardians are nothing but slaves,' scoffed Teasel. 'Your lives are at the beck and call of that blubbing snake!'

'You're quite wrong,' protested Umber. 'Our relationship with our snake is a two-way thing. Every year he sheds his skin. As he can't do it for himself, we Guardians scrub and peel it for him. Thus he gets to be bright golden again while we get his old skin to make into new suits and caps. And there's another wonderful thing he gives us . . .'

'I hope it's more wonderful than second-hand clothes,' said Teasel scornfully. 'I'd never wear cast-off clothes myself. It's like pinching other people's poems and claiming them as your own, as Meadowsweet does all the time.'

'The nerve of you!' bristled Meadowsweet. 'Thank your stars this is a sad and serious meeting, otherwise your ears would be briskly boxed!'

'Just wait till darkness falls!' cried Umber. 'Then you'll see the wonderful reward we gladly toil for both night and day. Amber our star-gazing girl is already on duty outside the cave. Later, hopefully she'll come dashing back with good news that will change our sad snake's mood into something quite different.'

'Different to what?' shouted the youngsters. 'Different in cheerfulness, we hope. His constant weeping for his lost tail is very sad, but also very boring.'

'All will be revealed when Amber our star-gazer makes her entrance,' said Umber with a smile. 'In the meantime I want you all to lift up your eyes and feast them upon the new cave-painting our artists are just completing. The mural is to honour our Great Golden Snake's coming birthday. His tragic one thousand years of sleepless nights and days without his tail. But look.' With a pale arm raised, he proudly pointed to a sheer rocky wall that directly faced the snake's unblinking emerald eyes. Harnessed to the ends of swaying ropes, two Guardian artists were daubing the final touches to their magnificent work of art. It was a study of the snake's head in all its majesty, complete with an imaginary body coiling through forests and hills, plus a masterly touch of genius. For the artists had painted in a tail of such beauty that the visitors below gasped in awe. Though the head of the Great Snake was golden, the tail far outshone it for glitter. Though the eyes of the snake were emerald green, the tip of the tail was studded with those real, precious gems. From an artistic point of view the painting on the wall of the cave was a masterpiece indeed. Though the tail did look rather over-grand considering that it had to be battered and tired after its hundreds of years of travelling home. But then artists had always had problems with painting the truth.

'That's exactly how the tail of our friend must look,' said Umber, overcome with emotion. 'That great work of our artists was freely expressed, and you'll notice, in vivid colour. Our snake loves it already. Just look at his wide, green eyes. He can't tear them away from his beautiful portrait. For it tells him how he would look if his whole body was completely together.'

'The Great Snake has no choice but to stare at it,' Teasel pointed out. 'What else can he see with his head trapped like that? Except us standing in the pool of tears, which makes his eyes go slightly crossed, I've noticed.'

'I'd like to ask a question,' said Foxglove, eyeing Robin. 'If our leader will allow me to? I don't want to be ordered up the rope like Coltsfoot for merely speaking my mind.'

'Robin would order no such thing,' said Fern, sharply. 'Ask away.'

'Umber,' began Foxglove, eying the small Guardian. 'We know you and your clan are good people who do everything you can for your giant friend. But why don't you gather your courage together and journey to find out what holds up the end of the tail? I believe you're keeping something from us. Something

27

you fear very much. What is it you good people are so afraid to speak about?'

'We here in this cave just do our duty,' said Umber, distressed at being branded a coward. 'If you wish to know more you must ask the Great Snake himself.'

'Oh, he can speak then?' said Foxglove, surprised. 'I was wondering what those small mumbles meant between his sobs.'

'He mumbles about mindless hatred,' said Umber sadly. 'From which he has long suffered from certain folk who would see him destroyed. But he will explain himself. Just be careful what you say. Question in a cruel way and he'll burst into more floods of tears. Remember he's a very sensitive snake who hasn't slept in one thousand years and is naturally very tired.'

'Very well,' said Foxglove. 'I'll begin with some gentle questions and very slowly lead up to some hard ones that need answering.'

'No you won't,' said Fern angrily. 'It's Robin's place to question the Great Snake. You're too young to get at the truth and understand it. With a weight of experience behind him, Robin our leader will fire the questions.'

'Oh no he won't,' shouted the outraged youngsters. 'Foxglove can question perfectly for us. Unless she's ordered home in disgrace as Coltsfoot was.'

'Let it be, Fern,' said Robin, shushing her. 'It's the answers I'm interested in, not the questions. Carry on, spirited Foxglove, I'm quite content to listen.'

And so in the hush of the cave of tears the questioning of the Great Golden Snake began . . .

Two

A Terrible Hatred

'Great ancient one!' called Foxglove, upwards. 'First I need to gently probe your background, which could be a tall story if you'll forgive my saying. If you're really as old as the Guardians say then you must be as aged as the tallest oak in the valley of our Willow clan. Which means you must have known that mighty tree when it was just an acorn. I think that's stretching your age a bit too far, Great Snake. So tell me the truth, exactly how old are you, give or take a year or two?'

'How old is the valley of the People?' came the whispered reply. 'That is my age more or less.'

'I'll ask the questions,' scolded Foxglove. 'Here's another one. We know you're an extremely large snake but how long is your body from nose to tip, give or take a coil or two?'

'How long is the journey through the lands of the People?' asked the snake with a deep sigh. 'Thus do I stretch more or less.'

'Please don't question my questions,' said Foxglove crossly. 'It doesn't help at all. As a pupil of Finn the great explorer I need crisp scientific facts in order to puzzle out where your lost tail might be. Your replies are very romantic but they won't help your case I'm afraid. Now, another question. Can you feel or sense your tail when you wriggle yourself?'

'I could many centuries ago,' mourned the snake. 'But we lost all feeling for each other as the distance between us increased. At this moment my tail could be here, there or any-where, though always in my heart. My prayer is that one day it will come home to me and we can twine together in blessed sleep at last. But alas I have bitter enemies. Foes who would stop at nothing to prevent my tail coming back to me. I am sure they are holding it captive somewhere. Which explains why my answers are so sad when compared with the crispness of your questions, small inquisitor.' And to the annoyance of his Guardians he began to weep again, large golden tears rolling down his scaly cheeks and plopping into the pool below.

Ignoring their angry cries, Foxglove refused to be put off as she wagged her finger up at the snake's snuffling nose.

'More weeping won't solve the problem,' she snapped. 'Name these bitter enemies you blub about. For all we know they could live in your imagination. Where is the scientific proof to back up your claim, Great Snake? I'm afraid your answers so far are cutting no ice with me. I'm trying to be kind but you're making it very difficult with your replies that smack more of romance than fact.'

'I think we've heard enough from you, Fox-glove,' said Robin, ordering her from the pool of tears. He took her place and spoke to the snake in gentler tones. 'Who are these bitter enemies who haunt your life and deny you sleep?'

'They are known as the Doomsday clan,' said the snake brokenly. 'They are of the People just like you but never so kind. Their histories tell them I'm evil and must be destroyed at all costs.'

'At last the dreaded clan has been named,' shuddered Umber, gazing fearfully around the cave. 'Let's keep our voices down. The Dooms-day people have eyes and ears everywhere, watching and listening.'

'Why do they wish to destroy you, Great

Snake?' asked Robin, puzzled. 'I can see no harm in you at all.'

'Because of their beliefs,' sighed the green-eyed giant. 'Their histories tell them that should my nose and tail ever meet it will bring about the end of the world in earthquake and fire. They believe that should my two ends ever entwine they would form a knot to crush the life from the world they think I hate.'

'And do you hate the world?' asked Fern. 'The question must be put, sad snake. For you have reason enough after enduring such sleepless suffering down the centuries. And we demand the truth if you don't mind.'

'Just the opposite, I *love* the world!' cried the Great Golden Snake. 'I'd do nothing to harm it or its inhabitants. I too am an earthly creature just like you. Even though unkindly fashioned by cruel nature to grow and grow forever, I still weep and bleed as you do. All I wish and pray for is to be reunited and sleep just once as a complete and whole snake.'

'I think everyone is entitled to be whole and complete,' chimed Meadowsweet. 'I'd certainly have trouble sleeping if part of me was missing.'

'Like your brain, for instance?' grinned Teasel. 'But then you'd never know it was gone.'

'This is no time to start another quarrel,' said Robin, as Meadowsweet bristled. 'This is a sad and serious matter and I feel we of the Willow clan should do something about it. Are you prepared to put your faith and fate in our hands, Great Snake?'

'I believe my fate lies in the mighty stars,' the weeping giant replied. 'But I thank you for your kindness, little one. Your offer to help touches my heart. But I fear that your puniness would prove as nothing when matched against the terrible hatred and cunning of the Doomsday clan. I'm awaiting the arrival of a special friend from heaven even as we speak. Soon the sky will be ablaze with his light and his streaking tail. We've often talked together through our long and lonely lives. Perhaps this time he'll return with an answer to my age-old problem, for his wisdom is born from the universe itself where all questions are answered. I thank you, Robin, but I must put my faith and my fate in the stars from where we all came.'

'Amber our star-gazer is already outside the cave scanning the sky for the returning comet that will hopefully bring good news for our snake,' explained Umber. 'It should have arrived ages ago, but even comets are late sometimes. It probably got caught in a heavenly snarl-up, what with the skies being so crowded with stars dashing every which way. But our Great Snake is certain it will arrive tonight. I mentioned the wonderful reward we Guardians toil for both day and night, Robin. Well, each time one of our snake's friends dashes down to the earth for a chat with him we witness a very happy snake indeed. From gloomily sad he becomes cheerfully transformed. And hopefully that great event will happen tonight.'

'This is all pure nonsense!' cried Foxglove,

outraged. 'What have wayward comets got to do with exact science? What use is a comet that arrives late? Anyway, stars and comets don't think and talk but merely shine. Their job is to guide explorers safely along their way. I'll warn the snake right now. If the comet is always late then its life must be one long lie.'

'My special friend would never lie to me!' cried the snake, gazing up at the patch of sky beaming in through the roof of the cave. 'When he arrives and we speak all my problems will be solved.'

'A perfect example of two great minds meeting,' said Umber reverently.

'Quite awe-inspiring,' breathed Fern.

'A shared sympathy across the vastness of space,' agreed Robin, very moved.

'But it's not science!' shouted Foxglove stubbornly. 'It's nothing but wishful hopes and dreams. When I get home I'm going to track down Finn, my hero, who'll be spearing minnows in the stream and roasting them over a twig fire. When I tell him about this cave and its weird inhabitants, and about the trapped head of a great snake who talks to stray comets, he'll throw back his head and laugh at the silliness of it. Then when he's stopped laughing, his keen mind will quickly plan a quest to the end of the snake's tail, using pure science, of course. Now I come to a tricky problem. I have a bone to pick with Robin. It's the same bone that Coltsfoot tried to pick and got sent home in disgrace for. My bone is that though Robin is a wonderful leader of our Willow clan I think he's too old to launch a quest to the end of the tail. Whereas Finn the great explorer is perfectly young enough.'

'How dare you be so disrespectful!' stormed Fern. 'First Coltsfoot, now you. Robin is the leader of the Willow clan and if there's any leading to be done, then he'll do it. You won't be surprised to learn that I'm ordering you home to the oak. There you can help Coltsfoot wash up the piles of dirty dishes in Granny

Willow's steamy kitchen. Off you go at once, Foxglove. And I'll tolerate no back-chat.'

'It's always a sign of age when the old refuse to listen to the young,' cried bitter Foxglove, clambering up the grass-rope in the wake of her best friend Coltsfoot. 'It usually means that their days of glory are over . . .' and she vanished into the shedding buttercups of early evening.

'Now we can talk about serious things,' said Fern, looking adoringly at Robin. 'Our patient leader must be brimming with plans to help the Great Snake overcome his misery. Come all the comets in the sky, our faith in Robin will not die.'

But the remaining youngsters in the cave weren't in the mood for more speeches that only made them more restless. The two sendings-home hadn't frightened them at all. Though they loved and respected Robin and Fern, those two grown-ups did tend to waffle on a bit. So it was with relief and enjoyment as they watched Meadowsweet paddle out into the pool of tears, her slim arms upraised as she gazed into the bright green eyes of the Great Golden Snake.

'Do you like poems?' she called gently. 'Because I've just composed one in my head for you, dear snake. It's about how I feel for you in your lonely misery, and every word comes from the depths of my heart . . .' and in her high melodious voice she began to quote, almost sing it:

'Oh how we wail
Oh how we rail
Oh how we hail
The end of your tail'

'Short and sweet,' grinned Teasel. 'And lacking depth as usual. Now, if asked, I'd compose a poem about the viciousness of that snake if he chose to bite us. Going by his size he could paralyse the whole world with just one nip from the fangs he keeps so carefully hidden. Then at the end of my tragic masterpiece all the People in the valley would be stretched out stiffly dead from his poison.'

'Our snake is a gentle soul,' protested Umber. 'He's never used his fangs in anger.'

'That's what all snake-lovers say,' said Teasel. 'Until they step on the tail of one, and reap their reward. Snakes are notorious for having short tempers. They always bite first and regret later.'

He and Meadowsweet then began a heated argument about the good and bad points of snakes, completely disrupting the once serious mood in the cave. The Great Snake began to weep even more.

'Right, two more for an early night,' snapped Robin. 'Meadowsweet, Teasel, I'm ordering you to follow the others up the rope and report back home. And when I get back from this meeting I expect to see the books in the library stacked fairly and neatly on the shelves. And be warned, I'll be carrying out an inspection later.'

The two small poets hung their heads in

shame. Their moods were black as they swarmed up the rope and trudged silently home to the oak now outlined against the spangled light of starry night. Back in the library they avoided each others' eyes as they went about their tasks. The only sounds to be heard were the thuds of books being stacked fairly on the shelves and the moan of a night-breeze ruffling the pages of Meadowsweet's favourite poems that Teasel had earlier swept cruelly to the floor.

Meanwhile back in the cave. With the moon shining in through the ragged hole in the roof, that place of tears looked quite beautiful in a lemony, spooky kind of way. It was suppertime for the Great Golden Snake. While his busy Guardians mopped his eyes, he was dining on a netful of freshly-caught silver fishes and a honeycomb stolen from the stinging bees earlier that day at the cost of many 'ouches' from his loyal friends.

'The problem is,' Robin was saying to Umber,

42

'Though I yearn to launch a quest to find the end of the tail I have duties at home. Our Willow clan is only now settling into the new oak and they need me.'

'Though Robin still loves a challenging adventure,' said Fern quickly. 'But it's very difficult with all his family problems.'

Before more could be said, a startling thing happened. A small Guardian girl came dashing into the cave through a secret tunnel that connected with the world above. Slung around her chest was a snakeskin drum. Looking very excited she splashed into the pool of tears and was soon climbing to the top of the Great Golden Snake's head.

'It's Amber, our star-gazer,' whispered Umber. 'She checks the sky every night in the hope of catching a glimpse of our snake's returning friend. If she thumps the drum once it's good news, if she strikes it twice it's bad. Sadly, for ages she's always had to thump it twice. But we and our great friend try to live in hope.'

There was a hush in the cave. The eyes of everyone were rapt upon tiny Amber as she stood poised beside the snake's ear. Pressing her drum close to his quivering skin she raised her fist and thumped down once. The watching Guardians sighed with disappointment as she raised her fist a second time. Then, smiling impishly, she bowed to her audience, her small joke over, her drum unthumped. At long last she had brought good news. A huge cheer rang through the echoing cave as she was helped down from her perch, the grinning heroine of the hour.

'Now you'll witness the wonderful reward we Guardians gladly toil for!' cried Umber excitedly. 'Amber has spotted the returning comet in the sky, the friend our Great Snake yearned for. At long last it's come back from the universe with gossip for our snake to delight in, plus hopefully the wisdom that will end the sleepless misery of our giant charge. See how already the gloom of the Great Golden Snake is lifting. Notice the change in him now that he knows that his heavenly friend is blazing in to visit once again. Oh, blessing on the comet, and blessings once again.'

'It's so true,' said Fern weepily. 'One always needs a friend, when one is at one's lowest. One feels for the now happy snake, one truly does.'

'I'm pleased for him too,' said Robin, smiling.

'And so are we,' cried the remaining youngsters. 'We're glad we weren't sent home for being impudent. The Great Snake's happiness is beginning to rub off on us as well. If the dancing and singing starts, we're ready for it.'

The Willow people who had only seen the sad side of the snake were astonished to see his features changing before their eyes. Gone were the tears. Now his eyes were sparkling like huge green jewels. His thin peaky nose began to twitch comically. Suddenly his grim lips parted to reveal the most wonderfully warming smile the Willow folk had ever seen, and they were all good smilers themselves. It was a smile of such bewitching sweetness that it swamped the senses of all who witnessed it. It seemed to radiate through the cave turning gloom into light, pain into joy, and misery into hope. It emitted so strong an emotion as to prompt the toil-worn Guardians into a frenzy of song and dance. The Willow people were swept up into the mood of celebration without protest. It was as if their minds were no longer their own. In the meantime, the Great Snake was smiling up through the hole in the roof of the cave, wrapped in a private world of his own. The moon had drifted away to be replaced by the glow of the silver comet, its long tail streaming behind. The snake seemed to be mouthing words to his returned friend, all signs of his former misery vanished. The dancing and singing People had no idea what conversation was taking place between the two giants for such heavenly events were way above their simple heads. All they cared about was the happiness of the Great Snake. As indeed he certainly was as he smiled and nodded and gossiped at the sky.

'Now we know why you Guardians are content to live your lives in gloom,' cried Fern, as she whirled in dance with Umber. 'These moments of pure joy are surely worth the endless drudgery of service you give your great charge. I must admit that my own senses are quite taken away to see your snake so happy. I've never felt so carefree in my life, and I'm not sure why. It's a strange feeling but I just don't care . . .'

'When the Great Golden Snake smiles you know you've been smiled at,' yelled Umber, prancing her about the cave. 'It's for moments like these that we Guardians endure the chill of this cave, the constant scrubbing of our snake's golden skin and the daily pain of being stung by angry bees. All those bad times fade away when a friend from heaven comes a-calling on him, and he smiles. Even you strangers are infected by the power of the Great Snake's joy. Am I right, Fern?'

'Why do you think I'm dancing, Umber?' cried Fern, dizzy with happiness. 'And who cares why?'

Alas, that time of merriment was not to last. The comet – for only a short while framed in the hole in the roof – passed away to streak onwards around the earth, replaced by mere mundane stars feebly twinkling. And the smiling face of the Great Snake fell, and the lightness in the cave descended into gloom again. And frowns returned to the happy faces of the Guardian clan as they began again to bustle about their thankless tasks, as the great snake began to weep once more.

'What happened?' said Robin, bewildered. 'Why is your friend in the depths of despair again? Didn't the comet bring news?'

'He seemed so full of hope,' said Fern, confused.

'Our friend is always filled with hope each time the comet calls,' wept Umber. 'But throughout the centuries the news it brought

48

was always bad. And now it's happened again. It seems all the wisdom in the universe cannot solve the problem of the Great Golden Snake. Now the waiting begins again, alas.'

'And the toil and the worry,' echoed his grim-faced Guardian friends. 'Until the comet returns again with better news.'

'The fate of the Great Snake doesn't lie in the stars,' said Robin, suddenly determined. 'It lies right here on earth.'

'Robin is about to make an important speech!' shouted Fern. 'And he'll need complete silence when he makes it. Order, everyone.'

'We're silent,' shouted the youngsters. 'It's the sobs of the Great Snake that are ruining the quietness.'

The Guardians rushed to tend their weeping snake. Soon his heart-rending sobs were hushed to wheezing sniffles and hiccups.

'Umber, people of the Guardian clan,' cried Robin. 'I wish you to know that our Willow clan will not rest until the end of the tail is returned safe home to this cave. If the stars can't do the job, then we of the People will right here on earth. I pledge this even if we have to scour every inch of the valley of the People.'

'Why should you take on such a task?' asked Umber, perplexed. 'Our clans were strangers just hours ago.'

'Robin pledges it because we're all of the People,' the voice of Fern rang out. 'And because we've fallen in love with your Great Snake even if he is a misery most of the time. He deserves to be able to sleep with the end of his tail after all these centuries of loneliness. And all of us yearn to see him smile again, for his joy makes everyone happy.'

'Except the fearsome Doomsday clan,' trembled Umber. 'In their twisted minds his complete happiness means death and the end for them.'

'The Willow clan will match those enemies should we meet,' said Fern bravely. 'We'll not be found wanting in courage.'

'And now we must wish you good night,' said Robin. 'But I promise you that when the sun rises in the morning the Willow clan will return with an expedition determined to journey and free the tail of the snake from the evil clutches of the Doomsday clan. This, on behalf of my people, I swear.'

'We'll await your return with fresh hope in our hearts,' said grateful Umber. 'But should you choose not to return we'll understand, for such a quest will be fraught with danger.'

'Better to suffer danger than a lifetime tainted with cowardice,' replied proud Robin. 'When the Willow clan rise each day we leave our fears on the pillow. Goodnight to you, Umber and Amber, and all of your martyred Guardian clan. The sun, I'm sure, will rise just for us, tomorrow.'

And on that parting note the visitors to the cave of tears climbed back up the grass-woven rope to the buttercup patch and the starlit sky above. As they wended home to their oak the tired but excited party had lots of time to think. Some believed that Robin had been a bit boastful, and had taken on a much too daunting task. Others believed he had not. Yet, to all, a quest to find and free the end of the snake's tail held captive by fearsome enemies seemed an ambitious goal. But Robin had made a promise and the Willow clan always honoured their promises. There would be no sleep for anyone in the great oak tree home that night, nor in the early hours. Before the dawn broke on the new day there were many problems that had to be thrashed out in the meeting hall hollowed inside their tree-home that had stood and grown for centuries beside the ancient stream.

Three

A Stormy Gathering

Throughout the history of the Willow clan one thing had never changed. As folk grew older they became more set in their ways. As had their parents before them, the elders liked things to be exactly the same as they had been in their own young days. They scoffed at the idea that the young could improve on the old way of life.

They shook their heads at any new way of doing something. In their stubborn opinion, all things novel and different weren't worth the drippings from an oak-sap candle. So the old were greatly relieved when the new oak tree home was built to look exactly like the old one they had been forced by the floods to abandon. With nods of approval, they watched the crafters at their work. The carpenters and the weavers of cloth and tapestries were pleased to go along with old advice for ancient ways of doing things appealed to their traditional skills. Soon the great oak was tunnelled through with passages and sleeping quarters, plus a great meeting hall complete with a cosy fireplace for the elders to gossip by. Great care was taken over the design of the kitchen. Granny Willow insisted on supervising every detail until it was to her liking. As a superb cook of wonderful stews, she insisted that the place they were stirred in should be equally perfect.

'A good stew depends on the contentment of the cook,' she would say wisely. 'And looking around my new kitchen I'm quite content to bustle in it.'

The gardeners had also been busy. They had quickly sought out the rain-filled hollows among the great boughs. Then they had worked day and night to pack them around with rich soil from the forest floor. In the soil they planted favoured flowers and berry bushes and aromatic herbs for Granny Willow to pick and dry. The birds and the bees and the butterflies were delighted. They at once began to seed and pollinate. Thus does a garden grow as good gardeners all know, and the Willow clan gardeners knew this well.

When everything was completed, down to the last bright hanging in the meeting hall, when the delicious smell of baking acorn bread was wafting from Granny Willow's kitchen, the elders gave their final nod of approval. Everything was exactly as it had been in the old days and they were pleased. For like old ones everywhere, the sameness was comforting to their ordered minds. And once again drifted the sound of the old songs from beside the crackling fire as this new life was moulded into the seamless, timeless one they had always known.

Yet there was a worry in the minds of the elders as they sang and supped their stew by the fireplace in the meeting hall that night. This was the absence of Robin and Fern and a number of youngsters. Coltsfoot and Foxglove, who had come home early, were questioned. The few answers the elders got were sullen and defiant. The small library pair were not in the mood for conversation. They were still smarting from Robin's ordering them home in disgrace for simply speaking their minds. Only scraps of information was coaxed from them.

'In fact I discovered a magic cave this morning,' said Coltsfoot bitterly. 'But then bullying Robin and Fern took over. Then they sent me home because they were jealous of my exploring talent.'

'I expect Robin and Fern and the others are

still pottering around down there,' said Foxglove, shrugging. 'Getting nowhere, of course.
For they know nothing about science and
modern exploring.'

The glum attitude of the two usually happy
youngsters worried the elders even more. So
when the absentees came dashing excitedly into
the hall to account for their missing hours the
miffed old ones merely sniffed and were not
amused. They were even less impressed when
Robin began to strut in an important way, quite
unlike him.

'Listen in,' he shouted, holding up his hand to
quieten the mutterings from the fireplace. 'We've
just had the most astonishing experience. So
astonishing that you'll be completely amazed.'

'The most astonishing thing is that you
deserted your post as our leader,' said an old
one sourly. 'Old Elder, our dead last leader,
bless his soul, would never have been so selfish.
He would never have dashed off on scatter-
brained adventures without telling us. What

kind of new leader have we chosen, I'm asking myself?'

'But you must listen, this is important,' pleaded Fern. 'We've discovered a cave under a hill that's almost entirely filled by the head of a Great Golden Snake. He's been denied even a wink of sleep for a thousand years because he's lost the end of his tail. Can you imagine how tired he must be?'

'I can't, I've never owned a tail to lose,' said another grumpy oldster. 'What has this astonishing discovery got to do with our family?'

'It's got everything to do with us,' said Robin, taking over again. 'For the Great Snake has been tended for hundreds of years by the Guardian clan who belong to the People. And shouldn't the People all stick together and help each other?'

'So how do you intend to help?' the old ones asked. 'And be warned, our bones are too old to set off on another adventure at our time of life.'

'I'm thinking of launching an expedition,' said Robin excitedly. 'A quest to track down the end of the snake's tail and bring it back home to him.'

'If you could only see the grief and longing on the poor snake's face,' said Fern sadly. 'And the worry on the faces of the Guardian people. I'm sure your hearts would go out to them as ours did.'

'I wish we'd never made the discovery of the cave,' sighed Robin. 'The sadness there was too much to bear sometimes.'

'If I may speak,' shouted Coltsfoot indignantly. 'Not so much of the "we" if you don't mind. It was I alone who discovered the cave of tears. *I* should be telling the story, not Robin who dropped in later. Why aren't you all crowding around me to hear how I jumped down into the cave to rescue the snake from his sorrow? I suspect Robin is desperate to get his name in our history books. Well I'm the one who should be so honoured, in my opinion.'

'You'll be waiting a long time,' retorted the grumpy elder from the fireside. 'Our Willow clan has quite enough heroes as it is. What our family needs is peace and quiet after the perils we suffered on the journey from the old valley to reach this reborn, sacred one. The last thing we need is another madcap adventure following hard on the heels of the old one.'

'Anyway,' said another elder. 'Why don't these Guardian people go and search for the end of their snake's tail themselves? After all, they're supposed to be in charge of his happiness.'

'Because their time is taken up just looking after his head,' said Robin, getting impatient. 'If they had the spare time to organise their own quest, I'm sure they would.'

'So they expect us to use our spare time,' said the elder cynically. 'They want our clan to pull their chestnuts out of the fire.'

'And get our fingers burned instead of their own,' shouted his old friend. 'That's an ancient chestnut trick and no mistake.'

'It's a very silly snake who can't find the end of himself,' said Granny Willow. She had bustled in from the kitchen with a stack of stew bowls hugged to her ample chest. Behind her tottered sweating Nettles with a large cauldron of hot stew which he began to ladle into the bowls, muttering swear words under his breath. He hated working in the kitchen when he longed to be a warrior. His jealousy knew no bounds as he listened to the other youngsters excitedly discussing the discovery made that morning while he had been polishing Granny Willow's pots and pans. He longed to join in the talk of adventure but his job was too lowly for that. As Granny Willow went back to her kitchen he dragged miserably behind. But he seethed inside. In a way the tiny boy Nettles was like a cauldron of the stew he served. Simmering. But quite soon his passion to become a brave warrior would boil over. Back in the kitchen he was muttering beneath his breath as he scrubbed and rinsed and sweated. His time would come, he knew it. His anger and frustration began to reach danger level though the placid Granny Willow didn't notice. When she did it would be too late . . .

'In my opinion, there's gross carelessness involved somewhere,' the grumpy elder was saying, puffing on his acorn-pipe. 'This Great Snake should have been keeping an eye on that tail of his. If I lost my pipe I'd move heaven and earth to find it.'

'How can you compare a pipe with a huge tail?' cried Robin angrily. He drew himself up to his full height and addressed the gathering. 'I've listened to all the objections and I'm overruling them. I'll now spell out my plan for the quest ahead. This night I intend to pick a team ready to return to the cave under the buttercup patch at first light. Coltsfoot . . .'

'Yes, Robin?' said the eager youngster.

'I want you to cross the stream and rouse Sedge our water vole friend. Tell him to swim and find Finn who'll be night-fishing somewhere along the stream. Tell Sedge to bring him back here. I've decided that as Finn is familiar with travelling with the stars to guide him, he'll be useful as my second-in-command.'

'Yes, Robin,' said Coltsfoot, grinning happily. He made to race away.

'I think I'd better help Coltsfoot across the stream,' said Foxglove, concerned. 'He's already fallen down a hole in the ground today. Being accident prone he could easily drown while swimming the stream. Now if I'm there I can drag him to the shore and pump the water from his lungs should he get into difficulties.'

'Good thinking, Foxglove,' said Robin. 'Off you both go.'

Soon there were lots of other eager youngsters begging to be ordered away on important missions. The elders shook their heads and gazed deeper into the fire. What was the world coming to when the young could not wait to dash off on hairbrained quests? they pondered. At that moment there were sounds of scuffling outside the hall. The sharp voice of Granny Willow could be heard, plus the defiant shouts of Nettles. He suddenly came bursting into the meeting. He was very furious for one so tiny.

'I know all about the expedition you're planning!' he yelled. 'Well, don't think you can leave me behind. I'm fed-up with being a slave in Granny Willow's clutches. I've spent all my breaks away from the hot kitchen practising my archery skills and I can now split an acorn in two at ten paces. I'll now issue a warning. If I'm not picked to go on the quest I'm going to run away to become a fierce outlaw in the forest, robbing the rich to give to the poor.'

'Be patient, valiant Nettles,' soothed Fern. 'There are still lots of things to be discussed and decided. Your chance will come one day, don't fret.'

'Coltsfoot and Foxglove have been gone a long time,' said Robin impatiently. 'How long does it take to rouse Sedge to pick up Finn and bring him back here?'

64

Then to his relief, Sedge arrived. Squeezing his plump body into the hall, he shook himself, showering everyone with muddy water. Behind him came triumphant Coltsfoot and Foxglove who also shook themselves in imitation of everyone's hero vole. After them strode Finn, his fish-harpoon firm in his hand, and an adoring Pansy bringing up the rear. Robin and Fern were alarmed to notice that Sedge was limping. He was supported by his loyal daughter Sage. She spoke sternly to Robin.

'I know you and my father are close friends,' she said. 'But that doesn't give you the right to rouse him in the night to do your bidding. He's been in agony with his painful leg all day. He was trying to sleep when he was rudely shaken awake by Coltsfoot. It's only kindness that dragged him from his bed to carry out your orders, Robin. I hope you're not taking advantage of his good nature.'

'I'm sorry Sedge, I'm sorry Sage, I didn't realise,' said Robin humbly.

'Don't heed fussing Sage,' said Sedge, smiling through his pain. 'She means well. As you see I've tracked down Finn, so what's this all about?'

Robin and Fern felt guilty and selfish to see their friend so ill. Sage was right. Noble Sedge should not have been disturbed from his sickbed. Rather lamely, Robin explained about the discovery of the cave of tears and the Great Golden Snake whose head was trapped there. And about the Guardians who devoted their lives to the Great Snake. Then he told the quietly listening Sedge about the quest he was planning to free the end of the tail from its enemies and bring it safe home to its head. But suddenly his adventurous heart seemed to fail him as he spoke. Sedge sensed the self-doubt creeping into the tones of his friend. His old confidence was no longer there. Sedge himself knew the feeling well. He was no longer the eager, dashing water vole he used to be. For time spared no mercy for the heroes of times past when their quick limbs slowed and their joints began to ache. Robin was sadly aware of this. The youthful opinions of Coltsfoot and Foxglove back in the cave had hurt him more than he cared to admit. Perhaps others were also thinking that Finn was the natural choice to lead the coming expedition?

He glanced at Fern. She guessed what he was thinking and moved close to take his hand, to draw him away as Finn stepped forward to take the stage, dark-eyed Pansy at his side. Instantly the excited youngsters closed around them. There was no unkindness in their action as they turned their backs on Robin and Fern, but just the eager turning of a leaf to see a new page. Then Finn the Fisher boy began to speak and question, his quick mind soaking up every scrap of information he could glean from those who had been in the cave of tears that day. They were joined in their huddle by Sage the water vole daughter. Robin and Fern just stood looking very much out of place, feeling awkward and embarrassed and knowing not what to do. Then

Sedge came limping over to join them. He sighed.

'Exciting though the quest might be, it's not for us my friends,' he said in his quiet, gentle voice. 'See how the young ones gather and plan as if we weren't here. Perhaps it's as well that tomorrow's dangers should pass to youthful shoulders. But don't let's be dismayed for we'll always have our glorious yesterdays to remember. We can recall, we three, the flooding of the old valley and the building of the ark. And the long voyage and the death of the loved ones we still grieve for. We were heroes in our day, good Robin, sweet Fern. In all modesty, none were braver than we in those terrible, fraught days.'

'I hope I'm included among the brave,' croaked the faithful magpie, poking his head through the rough-hewn window in the meeting hall. Though in typical, chirpy mood, his mind seemed elsewhere. Then he admitted he also had problems, though happy ones. He was now the proud father of two new eggs. But shockingly his wife had declared that their nest was a mess and in urgent need of rebuilding, and that she had no intention of hatching new chicks in the hovel they lived in. Sadly the magpie added, 'So you see, old friends, you won't be the only ones forced to sit this new quest out. However, Finn will be delighted to know that his expedition will be equipped with a brand new scout. Hop forward, my only son . . .'

With a sweep of his beak he nudged a small replica of himself into the hall where it began to strut with confidence. The bold chick soon pushed himself into the crush around Finn who were excitedly discussing the quest they would embark on come the morning.

'Why does age creep so quickly to slow us,' said sad Robin. 'We were young just a few seasons ago.'

'It's after sunset when I feel my age,' sighed Sedge. 'It seems the hours before its rising again are filled with pain. I often lie awake praying for the return of the sun, for its warmth to unstiffen my bones.'

'Well, I don't feel ancient,' said Fern, tossing her mane of tawny hair. 'If there's a prime time of life then this is mine.'

'Come now, we've had our days of glory,' said the magpie cheerfully. 'Beaks up, old friends, there's still lots of living left to do. I'll see you in the morning when we wish our youngsters God's speed on their journey,' and after a final fond gaze at his son he flew back to tidy up the disgraceful jumble of twigs that he called a nest.

'I too must be going,' said Sedge. 'We'll meet at sunrise, aches and pains willing. In the meantime let us take heart from one fact. Everything the youngsters know they learned from peering over our shoulders while we coped with crisis. A good grounding for survival, even though we say it ourselves. Good night to you both.' And off he limped to soak his painful joints in healing mud and to restlessly await the morning and its warming sun. Then Robin and Fern heard their names called.

'Come join us at the fireside,' the elders coaxed. 'All memories are here in the dancing flames if you wish to relive them. Come, gaze at leisure at the great deeds you did when you were young. Be proud that you have both entered the history books of the Willow clan. Don't look so sad, brave Robin, loyal Fern, for you've won your laurels many times over. Come rest on them here beside your loving family.'

Reluctantly, the two moved to sit among the circle around the fire. For a long time they stared glumly into the flames. They saw little there to cheer them. Surely they were far too young to accept old age so soon? While they gazed, they cast wistful glances over their shoulders. They envied the excited energy of the young ones as they babbled with ideas about tomorrow's adventurous quest.

'Robin,' said Fern, tugging his sleeve. 'Why are we sitting here getting old before our time?'

'I'm thinking that too,' came the reply. 'Much as I admire Finn, I fear he'll rush too headlong into the quest they're planning. He's too anxious to prove himself as a great explorer, having failed in his first attempt when we had to fish him from the sea all that time ago.'

'His coracle boat smashed to pieces,' nodded Fern. 'His pride too.'

'I think I can guess at his plan to find the end of the tail,' said Robin slowly. 'I believe he'll lead his expedition from the head of the great snake and follow its body to the missing tip.'

'Isn't that logical, Robin?' said Fern, puzzled.

'But if the tail has been travelling home for hundreds of years,' mused Robin. 'And if it's trying to complete a circle back to the cave . . .'

'It could be nearer rather than farther away from its head,' said Fern, his shrewd idea dawning. 'And you feel it could be nearer to home than we know?'

'It makes sense,' said Robin. 'What if the snake's tail is quite close to home but is being held prisoner in some secret place by the dreaded Doomsday clan?'

'Then break into the meeting and tell Finn what you think,' cried Fern. 'I'll back up your brilliant theory, Robin. If you won't go then I will.'

And she clattered back her stool by the fire and hurried across to push her way into the crush surrounding Finn.

'Robin our leader has an amazing theory,' she shouted. 'He believes that the quest you're planning could be going the wrong way.'

'There's only one way to track down the end of the tail,' said Finn, annoyed. 'And that's to travel from the head until the tail is reached. That's logical.'

Fern persisted. 'Robin and I believe that your journey would be greatly reduced if you travelled in the opposite direction. We're convinced that the tail could be staring us in the face if we searched behind instead of ahead. I'm sorry if I gabble, but the genius of Robin makes me trip over words.'

'Thank you, Fern,' said Finn firmly. 'I'm sure you and Robin mean well. But we have lots to discuss and little time to do it. Go back to the fireside and thank Robin for his suggestions. You must understand I'm trying to map out a very dangerous quest. A journey that travels forwards, not backwards. Using logic again, if the goal one seeks lies behind, what's the use in forging forwards as all proper expeditions always do? Give my regards to Robin when you return to the fire. Tell him I'll bear his amazing theory in mind if I can find the time.'

Very aware that she was being brushed off Fern stormed angrily back to her stool beside the fire. Robin wasn't surprised when she told him what Finn had insultingly said.

'Remember when we were young and thought we knew it all?' smiled Robin sadly.

'Now we know how it feels to be yesterday's folk, the ones we ourselves once scorned.'

'I can't sit gazing into this fire for the rest of my life, Robin,' sobbed Fern. 'And neither can you while we still have so much to do.'

'Just try to keep me here,' grinned Robin. 'The old ones are right in what they say. The flames of the fire do reveal things to the gazer. While you were gone I fancied I saw the tail of a Great Golden Snake in the glowing cinders. It was trapped in a dark forest by evil people, writhing and thrashing to free itself.'

'These evil enemies, Robin,' whispered Fern. 'Are they the dreaded Doomsday clan the snake told us about?'

'Who knows?' said Robin, peering into the flames again. 'Perhaps they're just shadows that exist in the Great Snake's tortured imagination, and mine too. Yet I'm convinced that there's sense in what I feel. And Finn wouldn't listen to you, Fern?'

'No, Robin,' sighed the girl. 'Finn and his

young friends think we're a couple of old fuddy-duddys trying to spoil their great adventure.'

'Then let them have their great adventure,' said Robin. 'And let you and I take heart that when they set off they'll have our stoutest warriors to protect them from the dangers they'll surely face. In the meantime . . .'

'You should see the sly look on your face when you said that,' giggled Fern. 'Don't tell me. Our boring moments sitting here by the fire are over. You are hatching a plan, Robin, for I know you too well.'

'In the meantime,' repeated Robin, smiling his sly smile. 'I need to look more and much deeper into the fire.'

'For more inspiration,' grinned Fern, catching his mood. 'More inspiration for the counter-quest you're planning.'

'Leave me some secrets,' frowned Robin in mock annoyance. 'You'll be kept informed as I work my plan out.'

'In my own meantime I'll leave you alone to

gaze into the fire some more,' said Fern, impishly. 'Nudge me if you need my advice, as you surely will.'

Not long ago the two had been close to despair to be shunned by the young to sit beside the fire with the old. Not anymore. Robin was back to his cheerful self while Fern was as happy as she'd ever been. The chatter of the excited youngsters faded to become a mere background hum as they sat quietly talking and planning together . . .

Four

A NEW LEADER FOR A NEW DAY

'I will now announce my chosen team.' Finn, son of Finn of the Fisher clan stood before the rapt group, his pale face now flushed with triumph. His green eyes sparkled as he savoured the moment. All his young life he had longed to lead an expedition into an unexplored region of the land of the People.

He had tried to forget his one and only quest to find the source of the River of Dreams that had ended in disaster. Now fate was offering him another chance to make his name as a successful explorer that would wipe clean the shame of his past. Now he stood with his sharp harpoon in hand, naming the lucky ones who would travel beside him through danger to triumph. He pointed with the tip of his spear.

'Pansy will be my deputy leader. She's loyal and brave, and if anything should happen to me the others will obey her commands. I'm also taking my pupils Coltsfoot and Foxglove. Should I fall mortally wounded during the quest their knowledge of the stars will guide you safe back home again. I'd like to take brave Sedge, but sadly he has a limping problem. So I'm taking along his spirited daughter Sage who'll cope with any watery problems we may encounter. We also have a new scout to spy out the land ahead. Like his famous father the magpie chick can wing for miles and alert us at once should danger threaten from afar. The rest of my team will be made up from the best archers and fighters who won't flinch should we be attacked by enemies along the way. Any questions?'

'Yes!' yelled Nettles, standing in the doorway to the Meeting hall and glaring. 'How about me? After all my practising I'm a deadly archer now. If you think I'm staying behind as Granny Willow's slave then you can think again.'

'Very well,' grinned Finn. 'Our expedition will be needing a cook.'

'An archer who cooks in his spare time, if you don't mind,' bristled Nettles. 'But you can call me what you want so long as I get away from Granny Willow's stifling kitchen and her constant nagging.'

'That's my team then,' said Finn, satisfied. 'I think I've got a balance of skills to suit the purposes of my quest.'

'Your team isn't balanced at all,' said Meadowsweet indignantly. 'What's the point of a quest without someone to record every step for the history books? Our valiant deeds would end up on a blank page for future folk to puzzle over. What this quest needs is someone with a gift for scribbling down astonishing events. So in the interests of the People I'm enrolling myself as the official scribe and poet of this expedition.'

'And I'm enrolling myself as Meadowsweet's official language coach,' grinned Teasel. 'Future historians would be confused if her account of the quest was garbled with bad grammar.'

'How dare you accuse me of using bad language,' cried Meadowsweet, stamping her foot on his, causing him to yelp and hop in pain. 'And if you try to peer over my shoulder while I'm taking down notes I'll smack your smirking face.'

'You've made a very good case for yourself, Meadowsweet,' smiled Finn. 'Welcome aboard my quest. As for Teasel, I can hardly take one without the other. He's also invited to come.'

'I think this quest is getting overcrowded,'

said jealous Pansy. 'We'd get along quite well without cooks and poets trailing along, Finn.'

'You must remember we're in the home of the Willow clan, Pansy,' said Finn gently. 'You came to live here from the clan of your wicked father, I from humble fisher-folk. It's only fair that the Willow People should play a large role in the quest for the end of the tail. Remember, we'd both be dead had they not rescued us from watery graves all that time ago.'

'You're so fair and wise, Finn,' blushed Pansy. 'When you explain it like that I realise how right you always are. You'll never be Finn the failure in my eyes.'

'So now, my chosen ones,' cried Finn. 'My plan is this. That early in the morning just as the sun is rising we'll shoulder our provisions and march up the hill to the buttercup patch and the cave of tears. There we'll drop down and question the Great Snake's Guardians as to the best route to take along his body to the end of his tail. While we're in the cave our magpie scout and Sage our water-expert will remain up top, ready to obey when I snap out orders.'

'And I'll snap to obey them, Finn,' promised the young bird.

'And I'll promise to do my best,' said shy Sage.

'Good. Now what else is there?' frowned Finn. 'Regarding loose ends.'

'Don't worry about details, my leader,' gushed Pansy. 'I'm here to smooth such things away. Concentrate on the deep thinking and I'll tidy up the bits-and-bobs.'

'Thank you, deputy Pansy,' said Finn graciously. He turned and addressed his assembled team members. 'My friends and companions, have we the will and the courage to face the coming challenge?'

'We have!' chorused the proud, chosen ones.

'And what if we encounter dangers that make our blood run chill?' cried Pansy, raising her clenched fist in the air. 'Then what?'

'We'll face and overcome them!' came the yelled reply.

'Now to our beds,' ordered Finn. 'We need what's left of the dark hours to get as much rest as possible. We need to be fresh for our early start in the morning. Sleep soundly through the night, we'll meet again at waking dawning light.'

The excited group trooped off to bed and tried to sleep. But it was hard to drift away, to lose themselves in dreams. For their wide-awake minds were awhirl with thoughts of the coming day, and the dawn seemed ever so far away as they tossed and turned. It was during those restless hours that each youngster had time to dwell on the awesome journey they were about to undertake. Quite soon they would be setting forth from the head of a Great Golden Snake to track down the end of its tail and hurry it home where it belonged. In their pride and excitement on being chosen to go they had given little thought to the enemies they might meet along the way, who would try to destroy their expedition. Now those enemies were uppermost in their fretting thoughts as they tried to sleep. How brave one could be in company, how afraid all alone in the night. Yet each one vowed before they finally slept that when times of danger threatened their quest, they would not be found wanting. Little Nettles had no intention of sleeping. Usually he slept in a cosy bed beside Granny Willow's glowing kitchen fire. This night he did not. While everyone else in the great oak had finally succumbed to sleep he was up and about getting in some extra archery practice. He spent most of the early hours pinging arrows at the pots and pans on the shelves and bowing to the imaginary cheering crowds each time he scored a bullseye. For Nettles longed to be a hero as much as he hated being a lowly kitchen drudge. Time would tell which role suited him better.

Across the stream, Sage, the loyal daughter of Sedge, was curled up with her brothers and sisters, also trying to sleep. For a long while she lay watching the reflected moon dancing on the rippling waters outside her tunnel home. She was well aware of the honour her hero father had bestowed on her. From her siblings he had chosen her to take his place on this latest quest the Willow clan were about to launch. Could she step into his legendary paw-steps and never let anyone down? This was why Sage lay unsleeping, watching the moon on the water, uncertain and unsure of herself. Meanwhile, high in the oak on a pile of careless twigs, the magpie chick was gazing at the stars and envying their gem-like beauty. How he longed to own just one or two of them to launch a private collection of precious things to equal his father's. And all the while the moon was riding away, making way for the bright sun and the coming day.

Five

THE FRIENDS SET OFF

Saying goodbye to loved ones is a sad affair. Almost all of the Willow clan had risen before dawn to see off the expedition. There were lots of moist eyes and many hugs were exchanged in the morning chill beneath the great oak. Some elders found it puzzling to accept that their children and grandchildren should wish to leave the comfort of home for a venture into the unknown. And, worse, with no experience behind them to call upon. Those old ones seemed to have forgotten how they also had yearned to break free, to see life for themselves in their own young days. But they took comfort in the fact that clever Finn was in charge and would take care of everyone. No matter that he had failed in his one and only attempt to become a great explorer when the Willow people had fished him half-drowned from the sea. His luck was bound to change on this second attempt to be hailed as a hero like his brave father before him. So everyone clapped and cheered when he marched his expedition team on to the parade ground of grass beneath the oak.

'What noble figures they all cut,' they murmured among themselves. 'It makes one yearn to be among them.'

Finn certainly cut a proud figure as, with harpoon in hand, he strode up and down the lines of his band inspecting their turn-out.

Beside him trotted black-eyed Pansy, a bow and a quiver of arrows slung across her back. She had taken pains with her appearance that special morning. She wore a forest-green robe and perched on her head was a jaunty cap trimmed with bright finch feathers. In the front row jostled Coltsfoot and Foxglove, Meadowsweet and Teasel, all burdened down with weapons and backpacks crammed with personal items and hunks of Granny Willow's acorn bread. Meadowsweet had taken care to tuck a sheaf of blank parchment inside her tunic, plus a jenny-wren quill to write with. The one who was cheered and clapped the most was little Nettles. He came clambering down the rope-ladder that hung from the oak and stalked across to join the rest. There was a fierce look in his eye that dared anyone to snigger. He sported a long-bow as tall as himself and wore a cooking-pot on his head. Granny Willow had insisted he take it, he being the expedition's cook. Tiny Nettles was hoping it looked like the helmet of a warrior about to go into battle. He was greatly relieved when nobody laughed but puzzled when some of the elderly ladies wept. Meanwhile, above them circled the magpie chick, anxious to be off on this first trip away from the nest and his fussing parents. Then Sage arrived with her limping father. After whispering into her ear Sedge nudged her to join her future travelling companions. Then, with the sun just rising over the eastern horizon, the friends set off, the watchful warriors spearheading the way. If the dreaded Doomsday clan were lying in wait they would have a fierce fight on their hands.

'Good luck, and journey with our blessings,' called Robin. 'Track down and free the end of the tail and make an old snake happy. If you fail in your quest you won't be blamed. If the time comes when you slump miserably on the ground and wish that Robin and Fern were with you, that will be understandable. As Finn will learn, it takes lots of experience to lead an expedition into the unknown. But Fern and I won't be idle while you're away. We'll be tackling the problem of the missing tail from the other direction. But you probably think that's fuddy-duddy talk from past-it elders. Well, so be it. Whatever happens during your journey please come home safe and make your family even happier than a snake with a new-found tail.'

'I echo Robin's words,' cried Fern, wiping away her tears. 'With all the love I have to give. Our thoughts will be constantly with you youngsters.'

'Fly fast and true, my son,' croaked the magpie proudly. 'And don't forget to bring home all the bright baubles you might spy along the way.'

'Be steadfast, daughter Sage,' said Sedge, his eyes a-bright with tears. 'Remember that when times get hard you're among good friends. And don't forget to shake your fur thoroughly after each soaking.'

'Just go and do what you're setting out to do,' yelled the whole of the gathered Willow clan. 'And bring back no tears and sorrow, just your healthy selves.'

Then there was nothing left to shout as the expedition soon shrank to small dots toiling up the hill towards the buttercup patch and the cave of tears.

Swarming down the rope into the cave, Finn was astonished by the weirdness of the scene that met his eyes. For a while, he and Pansy and the other first-time visitors gazed in awe at the trapped head of the Great Golden Snake, watched with amazement the Guardians scurrying to and fro about their eternal business. Then a yellow-suited Guardian came splashing through the pool of tears to greet them, delight lighting his pale face. But his smile faded when he saw the unfamiliar figures confronting him. He glanced around at the others and was only slightly reassured.

'We were expecting Robin and Fern of the Willow clan,' he said, dismayed. 'They made a promise to return in person at sunrise. I'm their new friend Umber. Who will you strangers be?'

'I'm Finn, son of Finn of the Fisher clan,' the proud boy replied. 'And destined to be known as the greatest explorer in the land of the People. Beside me is Pansy, formerly of the wicked Nightshade clan, but she's reformed of late. Please don't be alarmed, Umber, for your trust in our noble Robin was not misplaced. Sadly, last night, he and Fern decided they were getting a bit too old for adventuring. So Pansy and I stand here in their stead, ready and determined to track down and free the end of your Great Snake's tail, as are my chosen team ranged behind us.'

'Nervous Umber needs a familiar face to gaze into,' shouted Coltsfoot, pushing to the front. 'You must remember me, Umber. I'm the one who fell into the cave and discovered you all. Coltsfoot is my name, exploring is my game. Now do you know me?'

'I do indeed, young friend,' said Umber, his nice smile returning.

'And who could forget me?' challenged Meadowsweet. 'I'm the Willow clan poet who crooned comforting verses into the ear of your Great Golden Snake. I won't say my name for you know it already.'

'And a lovely poem it was, Meadowsweet,' said Umber, grinning from ear to ear.

'And you'll know the fool grinning over my shoulder,' said Meadowsweet sweetly. 'It's Teasel, of course, ever insanely jealous of my rhyming talents. Take no notice of him, Umber.'

'Take no notice of me,' grinned Teasel. 'I'm just the genius behind our mistress Plod who needs help with her spelling and things.'

'Well, our Great Snake loved Meadowsweet's poem,' said Umber firmly. 'But back to the problem of identity. Can you vouch that Finn and Pansy are genuine leaders sent in place of Robin and Fern?'

'With our hands on our hearts,' chorused the whole expedition. 'We're proud to serve clever Finn and fiery Pansy sent in place of Robin and Fern who are having trouble with their creaking joints.'

'You'll be pleased with Finn, Umber,' assured Coltsfoot. 'Even though he once had a coracle smashed beneath him he's fought to come back from that failure to lead this new expedition.'

'And Finn's brimful of scientific facts to make the quest successful,' chimed in Foxglove. 'He's on first-name terms with every star in the sky. If anyone can track down the end of the tail, Finn can.'

'In that case, I'm proud to place myself under his command,' said Umber. 'For I've been selected by my clan to accompany your expedition. I've packed a few things and I'm ready to travel. Where leader Finn leads I'll trek faithfully by his side.'

'Excuse me, Umber,' said Pansy, jealously.

'But as Finn's deputy I'm the closest to his side. Don't think that because I'm a girl I can't swashbuckle with the best. Anyway, you being so nervous, what use would you be to us?'

'Well spoken, Pansy,' said Finn hurriedly. He spoke urgently to Umber. 'So our journey begins here at the Great Snake's head. The best route must be to follow his neck and onwards, am I right?'

'The first leg of the journey has to be through the cavern beyond his head,' nodded Umber, shivering. 'Our clan histories are filled with the horrors that lurk there. I must mention for the first time the evil Scavenger clan. Down the centuries many of our brave ones have ventured into that cavern out of curiosity, but few returned. Those who came back were stripped naked and babbling about the terrible people they had met there. About those Scavengers who spend their wicked lives roaming along the length of our Great Snake, pouncing on folk who dare to brave the journey. The Scavengers are said to kill and steal for pure enjoyment. They favour the night and the shadows. From that advantage they attack the unwary and giggle as they strip them of every possession, to vanish into shadows and darkness again. With my scant knowledge of those dreadful fiends, I'm hoping I can be of use to Finn.'

'Perhaps we should go home to our oak,' came a tremulous voice from the back. 'Perhaps this quest will prove the death of us all.'

The lone voice was sternly shushed. Every eye was now on Finn their leader who remained unflinching at the news.

'You call the Scavengers a "clan",' he said. 'Does that mean they're of the People like you and we?'

'A branch of our folk who split away long ago,' Umber nodded. 'And returned to the old tooth-and-claw ways of savagery. I must warn you, Finn, we're bound to meet them in the cavern beyond our snake's neck. I just feel I can be of some small help if we do.'

'With those brave words, welcome to our quest, Umber,' said Finn sincerely. 'We band of friends would never turn away a braveheart like you.'

'Just let a thieving Scavenger cross my path in the cavern,' boasted Nettles. 'I'll split his wicked heart with a single arrow. And I'll also be close to Finn's side when I do it so he can award me a medal for bravery, witnessed by his own eyes. Then afterwards he'll sensibly make someone else the cook of the quest instead of me.' Then to his shame and the merriment of everyone, his cooking-pot helmet slipped over his eyes. Blushing furiously, he hurried to hide himself at the back of the group of questers. Would he never be accepted as an archer-warrior, he fumed miserably?

'Very well, braveheart Umber is welcome to come,' said Pansy. 'But only as a follower, as a useful guide of sorts. As I say, this quest already has a deputy leader.'

'What do you say, friends?' shouted Finn to the band. 'Is Umber with us?'

There were loud cheers of approval. Umber looked pleased and proud but he also felt afraid. Soon he would have to come face with face with the Scavengers of his nightmares. Bravely he hid his fears and smiled his thanks at his now brothers and sisters through the perils that lay ahead. Then he was urgently shushing everyone to silence. He was pointing upwards at the slowly opening mouth of the Great Snake. Suddenly the trapped giant heaved a great sigh, sending waves rippling over the pool of golden tears. At the same time his green eyes seemed to spark with hope in spite of the huge tears welling in them.

'Travel forth and be my ears and eyes, little ones,' he entreated. 'Search far and wide for the end of my tail for I miss it so. Yet I worry so for your safety. You'll encounter the Doomsday clan in innocent guise as you travel along my body, for their cunning knows no bounds.

Those people will stop at nothing to prevent you freeing my tail from their clutches. In their foolish eyes the sun will grow pale and die and never again rise in the sky if my lonely body should ever complete its circle.'

'I've been told about these Doomsday people,' said Finn, mystified. 'And they are of our own People. Why should they hold such ridiculous views?'

'Unshakeable belief in their histories,' sighed the snake. 'When a belief becomes a religion the heart grows stony to other opinions.'

'When I meet these horrible Doomsday people I'll give them a piece of my mind,' said angry Meadowsweet. 'In my opinion, you and your tail are perfectly entitled to curl up and sleep happily together. How could such love bring about the end of the world in fire and earthquake? Which prompts me to quote a small poem that's leapt into my head. I hope you like it, dear snake . . .'

'When your head and tail both sigh
Twined in snoozing stillness,
We will see the sun climb high
With not a sign of illness.'

'It's quite amazing,' grinned Teasel. 'Meadowsweet's poems are so bad they're awesome in a brilliant way.'

'Keep your jealous remarks to yourself,' said Meadowsweet sharply. 'The Great Snake loved my poem. See how he's smiling at me.'

'I did love your poem, tiny one,' smiled the snake. Then he raised his green gaze and spoke to every quester. 'Brave friends, I welcome your help but please don't travel into harm's way on my account. I have lived however sadly for a long, long time. Your lives are brief and precious. I implore you to take care as you travel along your journey. And should you fail in your quest, I pray you to save yourselves and hurry back safe to your families . . .' And then he surrendered

101

to another bout of weeping, his bitter tears raining down into the pool of tears where the silver fishes darted and flashed in the eerie light. At once the Guardians hurried to tend and comfort him, totally ignoring the excited explorers who were readying themselves to brave the sinister regions beyond the snake's neck.

'If I might intrude on all the grief, Finn,' called the magpie chick. He was teetering on the edge of the hole and peering down into the golden haze. 'But I'm still here and waiting to carry out your scouting orders.'

'And orders you'll have, patient scout,' Finn called up. 'You'll have heard that we're about to enter the cavern behind the snake's neck. I want you to fly into the sky and pinpoint the place where the snake's body emerges into the daylight. Then perch nearby, scouting for possible enemies who may be lurking in wait for us.'

'I'm off on a wing and a prayer,' cried the

joyful chick, soaring up into the clear blue sky. 'Beware my beady glare, all enemies of this quest.'

'I'm also here,' called shy Sage down the hole. 'Also waiting to play my role in your plan, Finn. I'm patiently waiting, trying to keep my impatience under control.'

'Dash over the earth in the wake of our sky-borne scout, sweet Sage,' Finn called back. 'Also seek the outlet where we should emerge from below ground. Prepare to help should we meet with danger here below.'

'I'll be waiting at the exact spot,' cried Sage, whirling on her paws and bounding away. 'I counted you all into the cave, I pray I'll be counting you all out again. Good luck, leader Finn.'

A short while later the group with Finn and Umber in the lead was squeezing between the narrow gap between snake and rock and entering the lemony glowing, echoing cavern beyond. Not surprisingly, the bulk of the snake filled most of it. Running alongside of him was a narrow channel, ankle-deep in the tears of his own making. The tears flowed towards some distant outlet. But where? Who could say.

Six

THROUGH TERROR INTO LIGHT

Keeping close together, the expedition waded through the stream alongside the snake, their only light being the pale lemon glow reflected from the dripping walls and roof of the cavern. Every eye and ear was alert for suspicious sights or sounds. Suddenly the party was shocked to stillness by furtive scufflings and splashings and high-pitched gigglings. Then a voice was heard above it all. A voice so dripping with evil that it made the flesh creep. Instinctively, the travellers huddled close to protect themselves and each other.

'Have you come bearing gifts, wealthy strangers?' whispered the voice from the mellow shadows. It was joined by other voices sniggering and mimicking the words. The voice taunted on. 'We poor Scavengers are always grateful for the gifts kind travellers bring us. What gifts have you brought us, we wonder?'

'A crust of bread and a fingerful of honey would be nice,' whined another voice. 'Oh, how my empty belly rumbles at the thought.'

'I wish I had a nice warm cloak like the strangers all wear,' said another voice, more menacing. 'Why are they so richly dressed while I'm so threadbare? It doesn't seem fair when I'm always cold and shivering.'

'I wonder what lovely things they must have in their packs?' sighed a greedy voice.

'How I wish I was rich like them. I wonder if they'd share their lovely things with me? I wonder if I could search inside their packs and pockets without them taking offence? I'd be very gentle as I searched.'

'I hope the travellers don't ignore us and hurry by,' mourned another. 'If they fled I'd be forced to chase them into a dead-end in the cavern and hug them close with friendly intent.'

'I'd kill for a small gift and a kind word from them,' said the first voice, wistfully. 'I'd be very sad if they were mean and heartless to us. So, my humble companions, let us approach the strangers with open hands and hearts and make our friendly feelings known.'

'This expedition is willing to be friends with all manner of folk,' called Finn, his nervousness plain as he peered into the gloom. 'I'm sure we can spare some of our supplies if you're desperately in need.'

But his words were ignored. Shadowy figures began to slide from behind rocks and from black hides to surround the terrified questers. Almost at once they could feel cold repulsive fingers plucking at their clothes and packs, could feel sharp knives slitting this and slashing that. It was done in stealth and amid much giggling as if it were a childish prank. The attack, for so it was, seemed almost gentle, such were the quick thieving skills of the Scavengers. For a while the friends stood hypnotised with shock as the evil ones went about their expert business. Then Finn came to his senses. Realising what was happening he yelled as loud as he could to break the spell so cunningly cast over them by these creatures from hell. At once the looters shrank away clutching their booty and snarling their defiance at Finn who had strung an arrow to his bow and was seeking a target. His actions prompted the warriors to snap from their dreamlike state and spring to their stations. Swords and bows drawn, they quickly formed a defensive shield around their friends. Suddenly some young questers began to wail, their voices filled with grief. Sprawled at their feet and lapped by the stream of tears lay the cruelly stabbed body of an archer, his bleeding body stripped naked of possessions by the cowardly Scavengers. A distraught Pansy knelt beside him staunching the blood as he gasped for breath, her concern mocked by the sniggering scavengers once more hiding in the shadows.

'We offered to share our things with you,' she cried, cradling the limp body to her. 'But your pleas for help were false, for you meant to rob us all the time. We don't care what you've stolen from us. I just pray you haven't stolen the life of this dear one of ours. If he dies I'll curse you all back to the wicked hell where you belong, you monsters.'

The anguish in her voice roused Finn to fury. Gripping his sharp harpoon he splashed into the stream and hurled a challenge. A cloaked and cowled figure stepped from the shadows, his eyes gleaming like coals through the rough cloth that partly hid his face. In his hand was a dagger still dripping blood from a murderous attack, in his other hand an ugly club. Could he be the leader of the Scavengers, he of the whispering voice? Whoever he was he raised his club and swung a savage blow at Finn's head. Nimbly dodging, the fisher-boy levelled his harpoon and thrust it at the Scavenger's heart. Blocking it with his club the other lunged with his dagger and stabbed Finn through the shoulder. The violent flurry had dislodged the hood that covered the Scavenger's face. The evil face revealed caused Finn to recoil in horror. He saw a bony skull stretched over with ivory-parchment skin. There was little nose to speak of, just a blob of gristle with breathing holes. The face was lipless and the mouth just two rows of mirthlessly grinning teeth. Finn was so shocked he was caught by surprise again. This time the whistling club dealt him a glancing blow to the side of his head sending him reeling back to fall and flounder in the rushing tears. As the Scavenger closed to finish him off Finn slashed upwards with his harpoon, slicing open the villain's face from scalp to jaw. With a cry the scavenger staggered back into the arms of his comrades, his now empty hands clapped to the terrible injury he had received. As Finn tried to regain his feet, another Scavenger splashed forwards. In his hands he held a leather thong which he swiftly wrapped around Finn's neck. Then he began to twist, to throttle the life from the fisher-boy. A sudden angry yell echoed around the cavern as a small figure dashed from the huddled group of friends to stand over the brutal strangler. Before the savage could finish his deadly work, Nettles had yanked his cooking-pot from his head to bring it down with a sickening thud on the Scavenger's bony skull. Howling with pain, the coward tottered back to hide among his ghoulish comrades.

'That crack on the head was from me and Granny Willow,' shouted Nettles. 'Think yourself lucky that my arm isn't as strong as hers, for now you'd be dead. Meet my firm gaze if you dare, or slink away shamed and beaten.'

The sullen Scavengers had huddled around their wounded comrades in crime. From time to time they shook their fists and hurled curses at the questers. But the fight had gone out of them for the time being. Seizing their moment, the friends quickly made a litter for their wounded warrior. Then, as fast as they could, they began to stumble and plash along the stream in a desperate bid to find a way out of that dreadful place. They were closely shadowed by the Scavengers who continued to spew out their hate-filled threats. Then suddenly, the travellers' hearts filled with hope as they saw a chink of bright light ahead and eagerly splashed towards it. At last their nightmare seemed almost over.

'Consider yourselves dead,' whispered a terrible voice from the shadows. 'Don't think you've seen the last of us. We'll be dogging your every step along the Great Golden Snake to take our revenge. And when our chance comes you'll beg for death, for release from the pain and suffering we'll inflict on you. A message for your leader, the boy who slashed my face. Prepare yourself for a special death. In the nights to come dream of my face and awake in floods of sweat and tears. Constantly worry, for I might come stalking in an innocent guise. Beware the twig that twitches when all is still, for I could be near. Gaze into the warming fire on bitter nights and see me there. Turn at the friendly touch on your shoulder and tremble to see my face. Be warned, stupid travellers, we Scavengers will always be watching, waiting for you to put a foot wrong. And then we'll pounce in all our fury to destroy you and your foolish dreams for ever.'

'Identify yourself,' cried Finn. 'If I have a mortal enemy I want to know his name.'

'Who am I, my comrades?' whispered the mocking voice. 'Speak it loud in case they should forget.'

'You are Scumm, our cruel and beloved

leader,' yelled his followers. 'And if we obey your every command we'll be rich beyond compare.'

'Shout my name again that all will remember and tremble at it,' snarled the voice.

'Scumm you are, and with obedience we shout it,' cried his cowled gang. 'Lash out at the world, lash out at us, but we'll always come crawling to carry out your orders, fearsome Scumm.'

'Hear this also,' came back a defiant cry. 'My name is Finn, son of Finn of the Fisher clan. I'm the leader of this quest to the end of the tail. Your threats won't shock me from my sleep. Neither will I fear you creeping close to kill me. You'll never take me by surprise. For I'll recognise the danger by your evil stench, gruesome Scumm.'

And that was the end of the exchange between the two now deadly foes. For the time being . . .

It was a hugely relieved expedition that squeezed between the body of the snake and the walls of the cavern to emerge into sunshine and a fresh afternoon breeze. Anxious Sage had long been waiting for them. As they filed from the darkness she hurried to take the burden of the injured warrior on her strong back, to carry him on to a grassy knoll nearby. There she laid him down and staunched the blood flowing from his wounds with a firm but gentle paw. The magpie had also spied the exhausted party trudging from the cavern and flew down from his look-out perch to help as best he could. Soon the whole expedition was sprawled on the grassy knoll that overlooked the surrounding countryside. Sage and the magpie listened fascinated as Finn and the others told of the terrifying journey through the cavern and about the evil Scavengers who had waylaid and robbed them of many of their possessions. They also described the fight and the revenge Scumm and his gang had sworn to take. Then Finn turned from that disturbing subject to discuss practical matters. He asked the magpie-scout for his birds-eye report on the lie of the land that spread out before them. Had the bird spied anything suspicious that the expedition should know about?

'Nothing to worry about, Finn,' replied the chirpy chick. 'I saw lots of dashing little sparrows and droning bees and butterflies raiding the flowers in the fields for a quick fix of pollen. Also a few hopping rabbits digging unsightly warrens all over the place. But they're all nuisances rather than dangers. So, my official report is that I saw nothing but boring tranquility ahead for as far as my eye could see.'

'So we can rest at last,' sighed weary, wounded Finn. He spoke to Pansy who was tenderly dressing his wound. 'Never mind me, see that our wounded warrior is made comfortable. Meanwhile, tell everyone that we'll camp here for the night now the afternoon is almost over.'

'Try to rest, Finn,' urged Pansy. 'You must be

quite spent after all the leading and fighting you've done today. Just relax. Don't worry. As your deputy I'll attend to all the things that need attending to . . .' and she hurried away.

'Quite some relaxing sight, eh Finn?' said the magpie, nodding his beak at the view spread out below. 'Some evening, don't you think?'

It was indeed. From their camp on the grassy knoll, the friends gazed down on a patchwork of green meadows ablaze with poppies and daisies and purple heather. Away in the distance could be seen an expanse of blue-hazed trees of a thick forest. But it was the sight of the Great Golden Snake that drew gasps of awe from everyone. After emerging from the cavern its enormous bulk wound around the grassy knoll before winding down through the meadowlands, finally vanishing into the trees of the dark forest beyond. The contours of the Great Snake shimmered like the brightest gold in the rays of the now setting sun. It was with reluctance that the lounging questers turned their eyes from the beautiful sight, for vital tasks called and the night was beginning to fall.

Soon a cheerful fire was blazing on the grassy knoll. The cooking-pot was snatched from Nettles's head and borne away to be filled with water from a bubbling spring nearby. Setting it on the fire, everyone then sat in a circle to watch as Nettles in his role of official cook took over. Enjoying the attention, Nettles peered closely at the water in the pot. The moment it began to simmer he reached into his pack and like a magician tossed in fistfuls of dried vegetables. Then turning his back he delved into a pouch he wore around his neck and took out a pinchful of something which he dashed with a flourish into the bubbling pot. All at once the watchers were licking their lips as their nostrils caught the scent of rich herbs and spices. The delicious smell suddenly made them feel nostalgic for their great oak home and old Granny Willow's cooking.

'Very secret ingredients,' he blushed. 'Which I

must guard with my life. Granny Willow said she'd clunk me over the head with her heaviest pot if I lost them. But I still appeal to Finn.'

'Appeal to Finn about what?' smiled his leader, his wounds bound and feeling much better as he relaxed beside the fire.

'About being an archer instead of a common cook,' flared Nettles. 'I've earned my right to be respected. Didn't I take your part and floor the Scavenger who was trying to strangle your throat? I think a girl should be chosen to make the stew in future. Like Pansy, for instance.'

'What's being a girl got to do with making stew?' snapped Pansy. 'Not that I can't. But my hands are full with being deputy leader of this expedition. And I'll remind all the doubters once more, I can still use a sword or a bow with the best.'

'So can I,' cried bitter Nettles. 'But nobody takes me seriously.'

'Yes we do,' said Finn kindly. 'Everyone saw how brave you were back in the cavern. But

Nettles, you're still too tiny to become a warrior. Just keep coping with the cooking and one day I'll see what I can do. And I must add, brave little one, your stew smells quite delicious.'

It was also delicious to taste. Whatever the secrets contained in the recipe, the stew was as gorgeous as if Granny Willow had prepared it herself. With acorn bread to dip it was a supper fit for heroes, and the hungry heroes got stuck in. Having been born a fisher-boy, Finn enjoyed his stew with added dried minnows while Umber dissolved a chunk of wild honey in his. Then with full bellies the friends sat around the fire and discussed the exciting and frightening events of the day. Later, when tiredness came, they rolled up in their cloaks and drifted off to sleep, leaving a small posted guard to watch through the night for danger.

After hunting out and gobbling down a few beakfuls of tasty grubs, the magpie flew into a bush to roost. He felt pleased with himself as he tucked his head under his wing and waited for sleep to come. Even with so little experience of life he was satisfied that he had done his duty as the expedition's scout. How proud his father would be, he mused, as he slipped into sleep.

Umber, the faithful Guardian of the snake's head, lay awake in the alien open air for a long time. He had never seen a whole sky full of stars before, and he was deeply awed. The light from them was so soothingly softer than the bright sunshine he had blinked against after emerging from his underground home. He pondered as he gazed at the sky. What was he doing here? What had he taken on? He had turned his back on his former safe life to join a band of almost strangers filled with a mission to find and free the end of his Great Snake's tail. Had he done the right thing? Umber worried. His conscience told him that he had. Actually doing something to end the snake's misery was surely better than just staying at home watching that misery increase. And there was something else. Despite the shock of the fight against the Scavengers in the cavern, shy Umber was beginning to enjoy himself. He was starting to relish the danger and uncertainties of a life outside his cloistered cave. He raised his head and looked around at his new, sleeping companions. He was part of their hopes and dreams and it felt good. With his problems thought through and joyfully waiting for the new day, Umber closed his eyes and slept more soundly than he had in a long long time.

Meanwhile, Sage was enjoying the delights of a bubbling spring she had found. Around it a deep pond had formed. Its edges were fringed with clumps of succulent watercress and juicy roots. After a hearty meal, Sage slid into the starlit waters and swam around in vigorous circles until she felt lazily tired. Gliding back to the shore she rid herself from the dust of the day in a shower of silver droplets. Then she too curled up and fell fast asleep.

Now all the questers slept except the keen patrolling guards.

'Halt, who goes there?'

But it was only a badger buzzling about his business.

'You, why are you shining those lights?'

But it was only an owl with the stars in his eyes, looking for sleepless mice.

Seven

A Strolling Stranger Calls

The sun was rising, the camp on the grassy knoll was stirring. Sage was startled from sleep on the bank of the spring by the sound of splashing and laughter. The early risen questers were bathing in preparation for the long day's march ahead. A while later everyone was eating a cold breakfast around the dying fire. Afterwards packs and weapons were checked as the party waited for Finn to issue orders for the next leg of their journey. While waiting, almost every eye was drawn to the wonderful sight of the Great Golden Snake at sunrise. In the growing light it was clear to see that his body hulked even higher than a fallen oak. But his shining skin seemed to twitch with life as no dead oak could. The friends marvelled at the sight of his enormous shape winding through the meadowlands below before vanishing into the dark forest on the horizon. Somehow the great snake seemed to fit the landscape as if he was a part of the earth itself.

'He's dying from grief, yet he lives,' said Umber proudly. 'He's old, yet still as young as this beautiful morning. For see how he lives through the life of others.'

Umber's words were true. The roundness of the snake's sides were draped with vines and lush green shrubs, shrill with the cries of nesting birds as they flew to and fro, gathering food for their hungry chicks. Bright lizards scurried across the golden skin of their host, snaring flies with their rapier tongues. A russet fox, his head and tail tipped with white, slunk from beneath the belly of the snake and stared hard and long at the nosy questers before loping away on business. With his going, a flurry of field mice appeared from their nests, eager to take advantage of his absence. A family of badgers, sleepy from a long night out, shambled down into the darkness of their sett, to snore the day away. As the sun rose higher, the hum of bees increased as they came out in force to gather the nectar that dreams were made of. All at once the slanting rays of the sun revealed a breathtaking sight. Festooned along the length of the snake, a million spider-webs glittered like precious brooches as their dewed circlets caught the light of the flattering sun.

'You're right, Umber,' said Pansy softly. 'I just wish the great snake knew of the joy his protecting coils give to others. For so many he is the whole of their world.'

'So much love the Great Snake gives,' sighed Meadowsweet. 'And gets nothing in return. The more I think, the more determined I am to find the end of his tail and send it home for a nice long sleep.'

'For once I agree with Meadowsweet,' said Teasel. 'This quest grows stronger in my heart with every step I take. I think we should approach Finn and tell him to hurry up this expedition.'

'Finn can't be rushed,' snapped Coltsfoot and Foxglove. 'Before we take a single step from this grassy knoll he needs to take some sightings from the sun to chart exactly where we are. It makes perfect scientific sense that if you don't know where you are you're bound to be lost. And being lost is the last thing we need.'

'Nonsense!' shouted Nettles. 'We can all see the great snake winding through the green meadows and into the dark forest. All we need to do is to trek along his side until he runs out of body. That is the spot where his tail will be.

Then after we've fought a bloody battle against the Doomsday clan who're holding it prisoner we'll return in triumph to our oak where we'll all receive medals for bravery. And when Granny Willow sees my scars she'll weep and promise never to make me wash dirty soup bowls again.'

Finn had been listening to the argument but thinking too. He had said nothing as the debate had raged around him. In truth, he was beginning to feel he was unsuited to be leader of the expedition. They had already suffered injuries back in the cavern, and that just on the first leg of what could be a very long journey. Had his decision to travel through that terrible place been a wise one? Yet even now the questers still trusted him with their lives. For in spite of the arguing voices around him he knew they were his to command. He was just about to voice his troubling thoughts when a stranger came strolling into camp. The startled people heard his song, long before they saw him. It was a polite and cheery song and everyone craned their eyes to catch the first glimpse of the singer as he emerged from the trees. Then the song got louder and finally they could see the singer strolling up the grassy knoll towards their camp. His polite and cheery song ended so:

'This has to be my lucky day
I saw your fire from miles away,
For breakfast I'd be glad to stay,
Good morning to you all.'

As the stranger neared the camp he stopped short and waited. Being polite, he was obviously hoping to be invited to join them. His song had thrilled small Meadowsweet. To her mind the stranger was a great poet and probably didn't know it. But she did, being no mean poet herself.

'And good morning to you too, nice stranger,' she gushed. 'If you've any weary bones in need of resting, there's plenty of room beside me.

Teasel will gladly shift and make a place for you.'

'Teasel will do no such thing,' said her scowling fellow librarian. 'One swallow doesn't make a summer, and neither does a ditty.'

'We all wish you good morning, stranger,' said Finn curiously. 'We welcome you into our camp if you come in peace. As for breakfast, there's some bread and cold stew left over if that will do.'

Needing no further invitation the stranger sank to sit cross-legged beside the grey ashes of last night's fire. Accepting a wooden spoon, he scraped the leftover stew from the pot into a bowl and hungrily gobbled it down. Meanwhile the questers were staring, fascinated by his strange appearance.

His hair was long and black and fell over his face like a curtain. He wore a long black cloak wrapped tightly around him despite the warm weather. As he chewed on a hunk of acorn bread the watchers peered to see through the screen of hair that hid his eyes from view. They were frustrated. Then suddenly a breeze stirred to waft his tresses aside. The sight was disturbing. The eyes of the stranger glittered black from deep sockets with a cold beauty. As the questers gazed he did not look away nor blink but stared right back. There was a remoteness in his look that chilled the blood. They were eyes that saw everything yet revealed nothing of the soul behind them. As if aware that he was being weighed up and judged, the stranger smiled. It was a warm and wide smile that never faltered. It was a smile completely at odds with the cold stare above. An attractive smile that melted some relieved hearts. Still confused, the friends turned their attention to his nose. They were glad to see that it was small and snub which meant he belonged to the People. Though from which clan was a mystery. Meanwhile Finn was getting impatient. He had been glancing at the sun and fretting about the passing of time. He spoke firmly to the stranger who was mopping his smiling mouth with the hem of his cloak.

131

'We hope you've enjoyed your breakfast,' he said, standing and shrugging into his pack. 'But it's time me and my friends were moving, for we've a long way to travel today. So if you'll excuse us, for precious time is slipping away.'

'I quite understand,' said the stranger softly. 'It's a long, long way to the end of the Great Snake's tail.'

'How do you know where we're bound?' said Finn suspiciously. 'Who are you, and what do you want of us?'

'They call me Stroller,' came the smiling reply. 'During my wanderings I notice most everything that goes on along the length of the Great Golden Snake. I always know when there are travellers abroad. And if they're following the contours of the snake it usually means that they're journeying to the end of the tail. When I meet up with those folk I always offer my help. I know you're anxious to set off through the meadowlands and into the forest. I've made the journey many times during my lifetime of strolling. Perhaps I could be your guide? You may meet dangers along the way and I know the shortcuts to avoid them. So, what do you say . . . I didn't catch your name?'

'My name is Finn, and I need to think about your offer,' was the cautious reply. 'I'll also need to consult the members of this expedition. After all, we don't know you well enough to trust you.'

'Consult away,' smiled Stroller. 'I just want to help, that's all.'

'Who needs a long-haired smiling guide?' said scornful Nettles. 'He's not even a warrior, for where's his bow or his sword? He just wants to tag along to cadge more free meals from us. This quest can face its own dangers without the help of this non-stop smiler called Stroller.'

'Over-confidence often leads to calamity,' murmured Stroller, patting Nettles on the head. 'Take care that your confidence doesn't make you careless, tiny one. Pitfalls await even during the gentlest of strolls through meadows. I know where they lurk, you folk don't. For a crust of bread and your company I can smooth your path ahead. Cheap at the price, I think.'

'Why do you stroll along the length of the Great Snake, Stroller?' asked Finn bluntly. 'And then back again as it seems you do?'

'Because I worship the Great Golden Snake,' said Stroller, his smile trembling as if he was fighting some deep emotion. 'He is the greatest wonder in the lands of the People. I feel this constant need to be close to him, to help in some small way to bring an end to his unsleeping problem. To end it all for him.'

'Such beautiful love,' whispered Meadow-sweet. 'I wish I knew such joy.'

'The start of a great sonnet if handled properly,' grinned Teasel. 'Just scribble it down, I'll tidy up after.'

Finn had been pondering Stroller's words. Then he spoke. 'The expedition will vote on it. Who's in favour of Stroller coming with us?'

'Because I loved his greeting song, I say yes,' said Meadowsweet firmly.

'Because Meadowsweet knows nothing about music, I say no,' said Teasel, equally firm.

'Stroller's eyes disturb me,' said stubborn Coltsfoot. 'I don't like the creepy way they watch us without blinking. I prefer to travel with friends who have bright twinkles in their eyes, not chips of cold ice.'

'Yet Stroller has a trustworthy smile,' argued Foxglove. 'In fact, I think his steady stare is quite romantic.'

'Umber?' questioned Finn. 'What do you say?'

'I'm torn between my thoughts,' fretted the small Guardian. 'Stroller may be familiar with the windings of our snake, but is his love in sympathy with mine? Does he agree that the Great Snake deserves to be reunited with his tail after all these centuries? Stroller says he wishes to "end it all for him". What does Stroller wish to end, I wonder?'

'Simply the snake's unsleeping state,' smiled Stroller. 'To end his miserable life is all I wish to do, don't you?'

'I'll accept those words as kindly meant,' said Umber, confused. 'Even though they're puzzling to a simple soul like me. My vote is yes, Finn.'

'And you, Pansy?' asked Finn.

'If it makes our quest less dangerous then I'm for Stroller,' said the girl, adding quickly, 'I hope my vote is the same as yours, Finn, otherwise I'll change it.'

'It's indeed the same as mine,' said Finn, satisfied. Then he turned to the small band of warriors who were sharpening their swords and testing their bows. 'What do you say, my loyal friends? Shout "nay" and I'll send this stranger away.'

'You decide and we follow, Finn,' yelled the warriors, brandishing their weapons of war. 'Our hearts and strong arms are yours to command.'

'That's settled, then,' said Finn, relieved. 'We have a majority in favour of Stroller's company and guidance on our journey.'

'Oh no you haven't,' shouted angry Nettles. 'How about my ignored minority? Aren't I allowed to speak my piece? Is it because I'm just a humble cook, not worthy to vote with the mighty? And what about our magpie scout and Sage? Aren't their views as important as anyone's?'

'My views being wider than most,' nodded the bird, perched in a bush nearby. 'Once airborne I can spot danger sooner than any stroller can. But as my wise father would say, always honour your leader and let his be the last word.'

'And your sensible opinion, Sage?' asked Finn.

'Glancing below I see a river cutting through the meadowlands,' she said shyly. 'And my watery senses tell me it's wide and deep. My task is to get our expedition safely across to the other shore. But if the company of Stroller

137

makes our journey more pleasant then I'm all for him coming along.'

'I agree,' announced Finn. 'Welcome as a new member of our quest, Stroller.'

Stroller's smile seemed even warmer if that was possible. Those who opposed him were heard to mutter that while his smile widened, his eyes grew colder. But they didn't press the point. Finn was their leader and he had pronounced on a fair vote. Only tiny Nettles refused to bow to the wishes of the majority, for he had a point to make. A very good point as it happened. He squared up to his patient leader.

'Aren't the minority allowed to voice their views?' he said, tapping his scrawny chest. 'If Stroller has been voted to come with us then that's that. But as a newcomer to our expedition I demand that he starts at the bottom as camp-cook. Which means that for a start he can take charge of this heavy cooking-pot.'

'What, and be denied your delicious stews?'

grinned Finn. 'Everyone would sooner starve, I'm sure.'

'I don't mind starting as camp-cook,' smiled Stroller. 'I'm here to help however lowly the task. I'll be pleased to cook supper tonight. In fact when we arrive at the edge of the forest I'll cook you a stew like you've never tasted before. And I won't need a pot to stir it in, for my skills are quite unique.'

'So I'm still lumbered with this pot,' grumbled bitter Nettles to the fond laughter of everyone.' How can I quickly draw my bow to fire a deadly arrow when the pot is clanging my head all the time? Sometimes I wish I'd never come on this quest . . .'

His moaning only increased the merry mood of the questers as they descended from the grassy knoll and began their march through the meadowlands. Finn and Stroller took the lead, talking and joking together like old friends. Pansy dragged along behind them looking sad and sullen and feeling unwanted.

She was beginning to dislike Stroller very much. On the other hand, Meadowsweet was delighted to have Stroller as a member of their team.

'It's very unusual to meet a poet and a cook rolled up in one person,' she babbled happily. 'What strange and talented folk one meets on quests.'

'I just hope his stews are tastier than his rhymes,' muttered Teasel, a step or two behind her daisy-hatted, bobbing head. 'For, somehow, Stroller rings false to me.'

'Shame on you, Teasel,' she scolded over her shoulder. 'Must you always look on the black side? No wonder your poems are always full of gloom and doom.'

Teasel's doubts aside, there was a carefree mood throughout that day as the friends strolled through the meadows along the contours of the Great Golden Snake. Ever lovers of plants and flowers the Willow people stopped often to sniff and pick the blooms and the fragrant herbs new to their eyes and nostrils. Each time they climbed a grassy slope the young ones rolled down the other side in fits of giggles. The river Sage had spoken of was wide and deep indeed. In the peace and the warmth of the afternoon sun it was a joyous challenge to cross. There was lots of splashing and cries of delight as the strong swimmers paddled across with the non-swimmers clinging to the skirts of their tunics. There were loud shouts of encouragment as Sage gracefully ferried across the packs and the supplies on her strong back. Even louder cheers when she clambered ashore with her cargo bone-dry and a proud grin on her whiskered face. How lovely she was, how lucky they were, the questers thought.

The trek continued into the late afternoon in the same leisurely way, everyone happily chatting away the miles along the creeper-clad curves of the great snake. Winging above, the magpie was also on relaxation station. With no hint of danger anywhere, he practised daring rolls and dives in the evening sky, glad to be alive when knowing that his friends were safe below. Then the blue sky began to darken as the sun slid towards the western horizon. The breeze had stilled and the air was filled with the cloying scent of flowers closing their petals for the night. The daytime journey over, the friends found themselves at the edge of a dark, forbidding forest with the plan to spend the night there. But how to enter the forest? Finn puzzled. For he was dismayed to see that the body of the snake described a sudden curve and now lay blocking the direct path into the trees. It was then that Stroller took charge.

'Just an annoying loop in the snake's tangle,' he assured them with a smile. 'We could make our journey twice as long by going around, but why waste time when I know of a shortcut? We merely walk under the snake's belly and out the other side. As I told you, I know this journey well. And by taking the shortcut we'll have more time to set up a comfortable camp for the night in the forest. I've noticed how tired the young ones are looking, Finn. Is my shortcut idea a good one? Or shall we go the long way round and lose hours of precious sleep?'

'Your shortcut sounds sensible,' agreed Finn. 'So, lead the way Stroller, and we'll gladly follow. I know everyone will enjoy an early supper of your promised stew and a good night's sleep.'

'I'll certainly sleep tonight,' yawned Umber. 'Having lived all my life in a cramped cave I'm not used to walking, pleasant though it is.'

Almost everyone agreed. It had been a lovely but wearying day. They felt they would tackle tomorrow much better after a bowl of Stroller's special stew and a good night's rest.

'A wise decision,' smiled Stroller. 'After tasting my stew you will all sleep like logs tonight. Just follow me a few steps more and I promise you all the rest you'll ever need this night.' Then he turned in a swirl of black cloak and hair, his finger beckoning as he led them to the entrance of an old rabbit burrow that dived beneath the body of the snake.

Eight

HORROR IN MINCING BLACK

Early that morning the travellers had marvelled at the beauty of the dew-drenched spider-webs shimmering along the length of the snake as far as the eye could see. But they were shocked and afraid by the sight that greeted them now. The entrance to the old burrow was spun over by a spider-web of enormous size. Each strand of the round web was finger-thick and vibrated as if finely-tuned to sense all approach. But it was the huge and horrible shape crouched at the top of the web that caused the friends to flinch and shudder. Mincing on its many spindly legs was a giant black spider, its pitiless eyes staring down at them. Its bloated body was covered in black, silky hair yet, astonishingly, it seemed to be smiling with its maw of a mouth. It struck Finn that the spider looked uncannily like Stroller, even to its smile. Noting the fear of the questers, Stroller hastened to calm them. Stepping to the side of the curtain-web he swept it open and motioned the hesitant people to follow him into the darkness beyond.

'Don't be afraid,' he said, his smile in place as always. 'The Black Spider is a friend of mine. He and his forebears have always guarded this short-cut to the forest. He and his twin brother only attack those who aren't my friends. But as you are my friends there's nothing to fear, is there? So come, follow me. You do still trust me, Finn?'

'We want to trust you, Stroller,' said Finn, confused. 'But the Black Spider frightens us with his smile. See how my friends shrink away from his friendliness.'

'When in doubt, turn about,' shouted Teasel.

'Don't be such a coward,' hissed Meadow-sweet, digging him in the ribs.

'I'm not terrified of the Black Spider,' said Nettles, advancing with his cooking-pot raised. 'If that hairy beast smiles again he'll get a crack with this. I don't care if he's twice as big and ten times as ugly as me.'

'Finn,' said Pansy, tugging his sleeve. 'I share your doubts but we might be worrying about nothing. We've come this far, we can't turn back now. We'll just have to put our trust in Stroller. Unless you think it's wiser to go the long way round. The decision is yours, Finn.'

'We'll take Stroller's shortcut,' said Finn, his mind made up. 'But tell the warriors and every-one else to remain constantly alert.'

So, led by Stroller, the questers entered the old

rabbit burrow. Instantly the smell of damp decay was sharp in their nostrils. There was only a murky light to guide the way as they hurried to keep up with the fast-loping Stroller. At first the gloom and the stuffiness of the place prompted jokes and giggles among the small ones as they raced to keep up with the leaders. There was much treading on toes and bumping into each other as they jostled to avoid being the one at the back with no one to guard his rear. Finn and Pansy increased their pace, determined not to lose sight of Stroller. Then suddenly they did. While turning a sharp bend he vanished from view. But why? They could only hope that he would return and apologise for setting too fast a pace. But he didn't. It was then that Finn stopped and tried to reassure his now crowded followers who had placed their trust in his leadership. His words did little to calm them. They could sense he was just as afraid and as puzzled as they. Finn felt Pansy's trembling hand clutching his, could feel and dimly see wide-eyed Nettles as the tiny one clung to his leader's tunic. A deep despair came over Finn. What a fool he had been to trust a stranger on the strength of a winning smile and a few friendly words. Then suddenly panic spread through the milling group. They began to shove and push forward, desperate to be out of this stifling place. Shout as he might, Finn could not control the panic. He and Pansy were swept up in the dash for the exit from the tunnel that could not be far ahead. Then the frantic friends could see light, glorious moonlight. With cries of relief they scrambled towards it. It was the exit, round and shining. But to their horror they saw that it too was spun tightly across by a thick spider-web. Like his twin brother behind them, the spinner was staring through eyes like chips of ice, his slavering jaws smiling. Then they saw the evil Stroller. He was outside the web looking in, his face pressed against the thick web as he laughed and sneered at the plight he had lured them to.

'Look around and tell me what you see,' he taunted. 'And see yourselves as you will come to be.'

'I see bones, white bones,' whispered Umber, recoiling from the moonlit, grisly sight. 'Oh, mercy on us all.'

'Death will be a mercy when my spider friends finish with you,' screamed Stroller. 'Prepare to meet it, stupid trusting travellers. Look about, for they are closing in, mincing nearer and nearer to you. Surrender to their biting clutches, for your time on this earth is nearing its end.'

'Not without a fight!' yelled Finn, brandishing his harpoon. His spirit spread fast among the trapped questers. Everyone drew their weapons, glancing wildly around for an enemy to fend off. With trepidation they had noticed that the moonlit Black Spider had vanished from the web. Then came the clicking sound of mincing legs approaching, plus a huge hairy shadow cast upon the wall. Then came a similar stealthy sound from behind. The spider brothers were closing in for the kill. In a desperate attempt to break free from the trap Finn ordered some of his warriors to charge the web and slash a way out. But their puny weapons made no impression on the tough strands. They were sealed inside the old rabbit burrow with no way out.

'Let me introduce myself in my true guise,' mocked Stroller through the web. 'I am the Lord Stroller of the Doomsday clan, and I make a fine stew don't you think? Enjoy its bitter taste, stupid innocents. You fell for my smile and my honeyed words, now pay for the trust you placed in me. Your quest ends here I'm glad to say, as does my day of smiling. Now I can scowl again in my natural way. Other pests will come after you with dreams to rescue the end of the tail. Once more I'll wander into their camps and grit my teeth to smile, to charm them to their doom as I did you, pathetic fools. I wish you all a long and painful time a-dying. Don't bother to beg for mercy.'

'We're not dead yet, evil Lord Stroller!' cried Finn defiantly. 'Your Black Spider friends will meet their match in us. One day we'll meet again. And on that day I'll be smiling when you beg for the mercy you refuse us.'

'In your dying dreams, failure Finn,' mocked Stroller. 'Prepare to join the piles of whitening bones you see around you. Before my friends scuttle near to do their deadly work I'll tell you a story. When I was small I swore an oath on the sacred histories of my clan that when I grew up I'd destroy the Great Golden Snake and all meddlers like you who'd try to reunite his head with his tail, the tail my people trapped long ago. But I in my rule am determined to take more drastic measures. I am turning my face from the end of my enemy to look him straight in his evil eyes. The new slogan of my Dooms-day clan shall be 'Destroy the head and the tail will wither'. For I swear that never in my life-time will the snake come together and bring about the destruction and the end of my beloved people. I'll leave you with a chant I was taught as a youngster. My clan chant it every morning and night as a warning we'll ignore at our peril. And he recited his chant while glaring in through the web, his eyes glowing with a fanatical light that chilled the blood of the trapped questers:

'Should the circle ever close
Sealed around from tail to nose
Then the Fates will rain down blows,
To waste the world in fury.'

'Think you never in your heart you could be wrong?' beseeched Pansy. 'Think of the innocent youngsters in our party. Have you no pity at all, Lord Stroller?'

'I closed my heart to pity the moment I was born,' said Stroller harshly. 'And now I'll say goodbye, poor trusting fools. Ponder my words as you meet your violent end. In the meantime, prepare for warmer company than me, for see

153

how my black friends smile as they advance on you.'

Then his moonlit shape flitted from the web, his evil laughter echoing on the night as he strolled away into the darkness. Satisfied that Finn and his friends would soon be dead, Lord Stroller was planning another appointment that he hoped would also result in death.

The fear of the fate in store for them was stark on the faces of the questers as the smiling spiders minced and sidled towards them from two directions. As they approached, the loathsome creatures began to spin out thick strands of shimmering thread. Their intention was clear. Some terrified glances at the piles of white bones still cocooned in silk was proof enough. The questers were to be bitten into a stupor, wrapped still alive in gossamer shrouds and left for the worms to reduce to bones. But despite the terror they felt not one of the friends refused Finn's order to form a circle of outwards-facing, bristling weapons.

'If we must die, then let's die with honour!' cried Finn, brandishing his razor-sharp harpoon. 'I for one will never go gentle into this dark night. Rage, rage my brave friends, and fight as I know you can. Not one step back is our war cry. Return every poisonous lunge with a blow of your own. If this is the end then let's die with defiance on our lips, and never the wails of cowards.'

There in the moonlit burrow a fight for survival began. Till now, Sage the shy watervole had stayed in the background, just watching and listening. But as soon as the battle began she shrugged off her gentleness and launched her tubby body at the clawing legs of the spiders. Though they were as large as she, Sage never thought to hesitate. In a whirlwind of soft fur she tackled the nearest spider who immediately wrapped his gruesome legs around her, his dripping fangs seeking to bite deep. But her own sharp, nibbling teeth quickly gnawed into one of his many legs, causing him to shriek with pain and tear away. Meanwhile every member of the quest was firing off arrows and slashing with sword and spear. First one, then a second brave warrior fell to the vicious bites of the spiders, writhing in pain as poison flowed into their veins. But though the friends fought valiantly the battle was slowly ebbing in favour of the powerful spiders. Twice bitten now, yet Sage still limped back into the thick of it, determined to sell her life dearly in defence of her friends. Then Pansy cried out as she was flung to the ground by a sweeping spider leg. Finn, also wounded by the flailing claws of the spiders, fell dazed, his senses reeling. Little Nettles fought as bravely as anyone. But he had quickly found that he could do more damage to the spiders by banging his cooking-pot on their toes. Above the screams and the oaths and the groans the voices of Meadowsweet and Teasel could be heard quoting heroic poems of past heroes of the Willow clan as they plunged their daggers into the odious bodies of the terrible Black Spiders. Words cannot say of the bravery of the others, save that it was awesome. But, though heroic, the efforts of the friends was not enough to win the unequal fight. Many fallen, they could only watch through horrified eyes as the triumphant, high-stepping spiders closed in to spin their silken shrouds of death.

Then, suddenly, the tunnel was ablaze with light. The smoky, flickering light from many burning brands. There came a fierce crackling sound as the web sealing their escape from the tunnel shrivelled before the flames. Then came the sound of hurrying feet on the earthen floor. Challenging shouts rang out amid the screams of burning spiders, the stench of their singed black hair stinging the nostrils. Finn tried to rise, to see what was happening, but his strength had drained away. He could only lie on the earth and pray that a miracle had occurred, and that the fate of him and his friends lay in kinder hands. As he lay in a daze he heard urgent words being whispered into his ear.

'Don't ask questions,' hissed a voice. 'We're clearing the lair of the spiders before we all choke to death in the smoke. Don't resist, leave everything to us.'

Finn and his exhausted and wounded friends asked no questions. They just felt great relief as they were lifted and hurried from the burning tunnel and into the fresh night air. Outside they were seized by more eager hands and bustled up what seemed to be a swaying rope-ladder. From below could still be heard the terrible screams of the Black Spiders as they roasted to death. Finn was anxiously sure he also heard the anguished cry of their brave, magpie scout, was also sure he caught a glimpse of that bird with one wing on fire. But there was nothing the fisher-boy could do as he was borne aloft, the fate of he and his friends already being decided by their rescuers.

Finn felt himself laid on a soft, leafy bed. Though his head pounded and his chest felt tight from the smoke he had breathed, he felt suddenly at peace as he gazed up at his beloved stars through smarting eyes. They were still there, steadily shining in their comforting way as always. Then he heard a faraway voice and realised it was his own, saying, 'Who are you, and where am I?'

'You'll find out in the morning,' came a soft reply. 'But for now . . . just sleep.'

Nine

THE PEOPLE OF THE FOREST

Finn opened his eyes to bright sunlight filtering in through a canopy of green. A girl with a circlet of red berries in her autumn-gold hair was kneeling beside him, sponging away the dried blood from the ugly claw-marks on his chest. As he regained his wits he felt suddenly vulnerable. Something was wrong, something was missing. Instinctively he clenched his right hand, his fingers closing on nothing. The girl smiled her understanding and reached to place his precious harpoon-spear in his grasp. Then she was gently protesting as the fisher-boy sat up and gazed curiously around. He was shocked to see that the sun glinting through the trees had risen to almost midday. He was angered to have slept so late as memories of the previous evening came flooding back. He was remembering the battle with the vicious Black Spiders and the two brave warriors who had been slashed and bitten to death. As leader of the expedition he should have been up and honouring their remains as they were lowered into the earth. And what of his other friends who had fought shoulder to shoulder in that terrible tunnel beneath the belly of the Great Golden Snake? Where were they, and how were they faring? The girl with the berried hair mopping his bruised face with a wad of green moss seemed to sense his concern.

'Your friends are also being attended to in our village,' she smiled. 'Just keep still and be patient, Finn, son of Finn the great explorer.'

'How do you know my name?' he demanded to know.

'You've been babbling it for hours, fisher-boy,' replied the girl. Then, gently mocking, she said, 'You must think yourself very special if your dreams are all about yourself. Twice you cried out that you were the greatest adventurer in the land of the People.'

'I must have been raving,' said Finn, embarrassed. 'I don't dream about myself as a rule. But now I'm anxious to know where I am, and what's happened to my friends. I'd also like to know who you are, strange girl.'

'I'm Scarlet of the Forest People,' she replied, offering a slim hand for him to shake. 'My father is Old Ashwold, leader of this village. We are the Guardian keepers of the Great Snake while he winds through our trees. One of our tasks is to brush him free from falling leaves and shedding skin. We also hold dances on his back to keep his sensations tingling. But I talk too much, pale Finn. Welcome to our village high above the ground. The Black Spiders are dead and your friends are being cared for. Here, chew on some hazelnuts for nourishment.'

But Finn was in no mood for breakfast. He got shakily to his feet and looked more carefully around. The sun filtering in through the green haze was explained. All about were the leafy tops of trees, their trunks narrowing down to vanish into the darkness of the forest floor. His eyes now wide open, Finn could see the village the girl spoke of. In fact he stood in the centre of it. All around stood neat little huts fashioned from hazel twigs and thatched with leaves. Bright flowers and ferns entwined each small dwelling making them bower-like and beautiful. Finn was greatly relieved to see his friends being busily attended to outside the houses just as he had been. With that burden off his mind he turned his attention on other things. One in particular. He had noticed that the surface he stood on was flat, yet strangely crinkly, and glowed a pale golden colour. Then something alarming happened as the fisher-boy stood trying to puzzle it out. The surface beneath his feet began to ripple and jerk as if suddenly alive. Without warning he was thrown to the ground as a mini-earthquake rolled under his toes. All around the huts were shaking and shedding leaves from their thatches as the shock surged through and rolled on. Then, thankfully, all was calm again. Regaining his feet Finn glanced at the girl Scarlet who had also been tumbled over. Seeing his nervous and questioning look she smiled, gracefully rising and brushing the leaves from her autumn hair.

'It's a problem we Forest folk are used to,' she explained. 'Living on top of our Great Snake's back, we take his shivers in our stride. But up here we're safe from our enemies who skulk the forest floor. I speak of Lord Stroller and his clan in particular. You've met him, of course. Last night we triumphed against his evil plotting for the very first time. We knew another expedition was on its way to free the end of the tail. We sensed our snake's excitement through the ripples along his skin, for we long ago learned to read such messages. So when you and your friends were lured by Stroller into the lair of the Black Spiders we were prepared and ready to thwart his plans this time. And we Forest People did, for here you are safe and sound in our village on the Great Snake's back.'

'All except for our two dead warriors,' said Finn sadly. 'Who gave their lives that the rest of us might live.'

'Never forgetting those,' said Scarlet, bowing her pretty head.

'So we questers have a lot to thank your people for,' said Finn. 'And I do on behalf of myself and my friends.'

'You should really thank my father, Old Ash-wold,' said Scarlet. 'He's our chief and the rescue plan was his. But you'll be meeting him quite soon.'

'I'll be honoured to,' grinned Finn, his strength and humour returning. 'And if he's as wise as his daughter is beautiful, he must be quite a chief.'

Scarlet blushed as redly as the berries in her hair. But she hid her pleasure for she had serious words to say. 'Never forget the threat Lord Stroller still poses, Finn. At this moment he probably thinks you're all dead. When he finds out that you still live he'll strike again with even more fury. Stroller being the obsessed soul that he is, he'll prevent you reaching the end of the tail if he dies in the attempt. For such is the hatred of the Doomsday clan for our sleepless giant whose only crime is to yearn for his tail to come home.'

'There's also the Scavengers to worry about,' said Finn, his fingers tightening around his harpoon. 'Especially their leader Scumm who's sworn a personal vendetta against me. We fought back in the cavern where I deeply scarred his face and his pride.'

'You've tangled with the odious Scavengers?' whispered Scarlet, horrified. 'Oh, Finn, how I fear for you with all the dangers you must face. Looking at you just standing there, alone and palely loitering breaks my heart. Yet I know that your puny body is filled with an inner strength.'

'Loitering? Puny?' said Finn indignantly, flexing his muscles. 'I'll have you know I've never loitered in my life. I have too much important exploring to do. Let my enemies close around me as they will. I'll face them with this trusty blade and a face as harsh as stone.'

'I watched your face all through the night, brave Finn,' said Scarlet gently. 'I saw no trace of harshness there. Yet even the blooded warrior is entitled to sleep in peace . . . even sweetly as you were.'

They were interrupted as members of the expedition began to drift over, some limping and leaning on friends, most of them bearing the slashes and bruises earned from the battle with the spiders. There was sadness in the eyes of everyone, but not for themselves. Their grief was for the two valiant fighters they had lost. Soon they were all standing around Finn waiting for him to speak. He did, his tone grave but confident.

'This is a sad morning for us,' he began. 'Yet we should feel a little bit happy, thanks to the Forest People who saved our lives last night. As for myself, I accept full blame for leading you into the spider-trap that Stroller had prepared for us. If you have lost your faith in me as your leader and wish to go home to our valley then do so, and with my blessing. I only know that when I'm fully healed and fit again I intend to go on to the end of the tail. I won't ask for company. You can come or you can go, it's up to you my friends. But in the meantime our fallen friends must be buried with full honours in the forest earth below. They died for us, let us pray for them with all of our hearts.'

'The burying is done, Finn,' said Coltsfoot quietly. 'Some of us rose early and climbed down the rope-ladder to wrap our friends in their cloaks and dig their graves. We chose not to wake you. Your snores were so peaceful after the hard fighting you've done. I for one still have every faith in you. We all know by now that quests can be filled with danger as well as excitement. In spite of our loss I still believe that most of us wish to journey on to complete our quest for the end of the tail.'

'Even if it leads to the end of our own tale in death,' cried a voice from among the friends. 'This tale started at the beginning and will finish at the end. What fools would we look like if we stopped in the middle with the end of neither the snake's tail nor our own tale reached?'

'I don't know what that means,' said Meadowsweet, inspired. 'But I'm jotting it down in my journal to make into a beautiful poem.'

'Sense into rubbish, rubbish into sense,' grinned Teasel. 'You've always been good at that. Don't worry about the spelling mistakes, I'll tidy them later!'

'Do you know what the word "boring" means?' replied Meadowsweet icily. 'As it spells "Teasel" you'll find it at the top of your good spelling guide.'

They were frowned at and quickly pulled apart before an arguement spoiled the serious tone of the meeting.

'We early risers would have roused you, Finn,' explained Foxglove. 'But you were sleeping so sweetly in the care of the girl with red berries in her hair. Don't worry, I laid a special bunch of flowers on the graves as if they had come from you.'

'And I quoted a simple poem as they were lowered into the earth,' said Meadowsweet, brushing a tear from her eye.

'And wonderfully simple it was,' said Teasel, kindly patting her heaving shoulders. 'I was there and I heard it. But I think due credit should go to Sage who solemnly dug the graves with her strong paws. And to our magpie scout perched gravely on a twig above looking splendid in his black-and-white mourning. Even though his wings were badly singed in the battle last night he refused to squawk in agony. For the sad occasion he kept his pain buttoned behind his stiff, upper-lip beak.'

'Oh, it was nothing,' winced the magpie from the thatch of a hut nearby. 'And feathers always grow again, I hope.'

'And I banged a drum in time with the slow march,' shouted Nettles proudly. 'Even though it was only my cooking-pot muffled with moss. The problem is, I've left my pot down there, and I'll soon have stew to prepare. Remind me to nip back down to earth and get it. Granny Willow will skin me alive if I lose one of her pots.'

'I'm proud of you all,' said Finn, glad to have such friends. 'I just hope that one day you'll be truly proud of me.'

Just then a heroine water vole came limping towards them, a shy grin on her whiskered face.

Modestly brushing aside Finn's thanks for her bravery, she gently teased him for sleeping so late while the rest of the world was bustling. But everyone knew she was masking much pain with her joke. None more than Sage had suffered during the fight against the loathsome spider brothers. Then suddenly an angry voice was heard and Pansy came storming from a nearby hut. She wore a bloody bandage around her head and her eyes flashed fire as she saw Scarlet standing by Finn's side. When she was told that the girl with the berries was merely Finn's devoted nurse she snorted, but calmed a little. Then another quest member came hobbling over to join them. It was Umber and he was warmly welcomed, even cheered.

'I'm sorry I'm not a born fighter, my friends,' he apologised. 'I did my best in the desperate hours last night, but my best wasn't good enough. I managed to stamp on some spider toes but I wish I'd done more. I would gladly have died in the place of those brave warriors, but I just wasn't up to it. I wanted to fight but I just kept being pushed out of the way each time I tried.'

'You were loyal, that's the important thing, Umber,' Finn comforted. 'That's why you were cheered when you appeared. Better a friend who would die for friends than a coward who dies for himself.'

'No lofty praise for me, I notice,' remarked the bitter magpie. 'A few words of thanks is all I've had. I've kept my beak stiffly buttoned up till now. So who cares that my wings were singed during the battle and I can scarcely flutter? Why should you care that I battered my head against the spider-web trying to get in to help you? Why should you care that I constantly flew guard while you were being rescued from the blazing tunnel? What's it to Finn that I was attending this morning's burial service while he lay snoring in bed?'

'And we praise you from our hearts, noble bird,' said Finn sincerely.

'I haven't finished yet,' snapped the magpie crossly. 'I've lots more to get off my singed chest. For instance, sometimes I feel I'm only a servant in your eyes, just a bird you use to scout ahead to smooth your path. Well let me tell you something about the scouting business. Many times I've been swooped on by hungry hawks while spying out the land ahead for this quest. Sometimes I feared that my eyes and my wings would give out from the gruelling hours I've spent aloft for you. But I don't want your praise, ungrateful friends. I beg and implore you not to praise me for I'm used to being treated with contempt.'

'Too late, brave bird,' smiled Finn. 'You've already been praised. But you don't need to fish for compliments. I'll only say that your worth to this quest is precious and you know it. So spare us the hurt, beady-eyed look. You know we all count and dote and depend on you.'

'Then show it more,' said the ruffled bird, though looking very pleased. 'I accept your humble apology, Finn. In future, be quicker with the praise and we'll get along much better.'

'Three cheers for the singed magpie who's put Finn in his place,' shouted Nettles. 'I also know how it feels to be scorned by our unfeeling leader. But you'll have to cheer without me for I'm off down the rope-ladder to pick up my drumming-pot from the graveside of our heroes.'

The cheers were few and ragged as he hurried away. For all attention was suddenly drawn to a small group of people approaching. At their head was a tall and majestic figure wearing a colourful robe of dried leaves of every seasonal hue. The curious could pick out the evergreens of winter, the pushy pale of spring, the languid of summer and the red-gold of autumn, all celebrated in a cloak around the shoulders of one frail old man. His brow was adorned with a crown of woodland seeds, and in his gnarled hand he carried a twisted staff that was strangely in bud despite its age. He could only be the chief of the Forest People, Old Ashwold. The slim girl Scarlet hurried to kiss his cheek in affectionate greeting.

'Welcome to our forest home,' smiled Old Ashwold as Finn stepped forward. 'You'll be the fisher-boy in charge of this quest to the end of the Great Golden Snake. I've been hearing a lot about you. My daughter has told you about our defeating of the Black Spiders last night. We Forest People were determined that your expedition wouldn't suffer the fate of the ones before you. This time we vowed that Lord Stroller and his Doomsday clan would not triumph. Now the Black Spiders are no more, thanks to the courage and the blazing torches of my people. And now, Finn, you and your friends are standing where all past quests have never stood before. With the spider-trap behind you, the way is clear to continue your quest to the end of the tail, and free it. You and your friends can be sure that your journey through our forest will be a safe one. But only to the farther edge, I must warn you. For beyond our green home lies The Wilderness through which our Great Snake winds. That terrible place is the haunt of the Scavengers who slink through the mists and wallow in the stinking swamps there. A retreat where they store their stolen booty and hold for ransom the innocent travellers they kidnap. We will take you to the place where our tree-line ends, Finn, but no farther. The fear our histories fill us with is far too great to overcome. We only know there are Guardians out there in The Wilderness, God help them. We can only pass you on to them and pray for you.'

'We understand, Old Ashwold,' said Finn soberly. 'It's our dangerous quest and not yours, after all.'

'But for this day you and your friends must rest after your ordeal,' smiled the old forest leader. 'Tonight we'll have a feast and a dance in your honour.'

'And we'll be honoured to attend,' said Finn gratefully. 'Our expedition will be happy to relax for a while.'

'We dance all night at our feasts, Finn,' said Scarlet, her eyes shining. 'Sometimes even till dawn.'

'Finn won't have time for such nonsense,' snapped Pansy. 'Tonight he'll be studying the stars and plotting our route along the snake through The Wilderness. Many lives will hang on his expert judgement. Dancing and cavorting indeed . . .'

'And now I wish to meet and embrace my kinsman from the cave of tears,' said Old Ashwold. 'Where is he?'

'Here I am, great chief,' said Umber, shyly stepping forward. He was immediately crushed against the oldster's leafy chest.

'Come, we have lots to talk about, we Guardians of the Great Golden Snake,' beamed Old Ashwold, leading breathless and bewildered Umber away to his hut to chat about their clan histories.

'I hope Umber has a head for strong chestnut punch,' said Scarlet, concerned. 'Because my father drinks lots of it. I fear that quiet Umber will become quite merry before this day and night is out.'

'We all deserve to be merry for a while,' cried Meadowsweet. 'We've had sorrow enough since setting out on this quest. Our dead warriors have been buried with love. I'm sure their souls would wish us to enjoy ourselves while we can. For myself, I'm going to whirl and dance at the celebrations tonight. I'll even dance with Teasel if he asks me nicely.'

'Don't build up your hopes,' grinned Teasel. 'I'll be much too busy dancing the night away with the beautiful forest girls. But I'll keep you in mind if I run out of partners.'

'You conceited oaf,' fumed Meadowsweet, stamping her foot and storming away. 'I'd sooner dance with a hairy Black Spider than you.'

'Now what have I said?' asked Teasel innocently.

'Too much as usual,' said Pansy, frowning. 'You know how sensitive she is.'

'I'll try to remember in future,' said Teasel, grinning again.

Ten

Our Cook and his Pot are Missing

It was during the moonlit feast and the dancing when someone mentioned that Nettles was missing. Though Finn had drunk plenty of chestnut punch and had danced happily with both Scarlet and Pansy his mind had remained alert. At once he began to fire questions. When had Nettles last been seen, and where? Why hadn't his absence been reported sooner? Where could he possibly be? Then someone remembered and quoted the last words of the small cook before he had hurried away somewhere: 'But you'll have to cheer without me for I'm off down the rope-ladder to pick up my drumming-pot from the gravesides of our heroes.'

Since then there had been no sight nor sound of him, which was strange. Nettles had always loved to be in the thick of things. He would have pushed himself into the limelight of the feast and the dance, even though past his bedtime. But he wasn't here, and never had been . . .

Immediately Finn began to snap out orders for a search to be mounted throughout the village. The Forest folk were just as concerned, and only too willing to help. Just as small search parties were about to set out, an evil voice came echoing up from the forest floor. It was a voice that chilled the blood of the listeners and was hatefully familiar.

'Peer down and behold your tiny missing

cook,' sneered the voice of Scumm. 'In case you can't see through the darkness, I'm holding his squirming body up by the ankles. If you don't believe me I'll just give my prisoner a sharp tweak.'

'Ouch, and ouch again!' yelled a voice that could only be Nettles. 'That wasn't fair, you kidnapping Scumm. You tweaked both my ears. But torture away, tweak every part of me. As a warrior I'm noble enough to bear the pain without crying. As for my ransom, I refuse to pay it. And you're certainly not having my cooking-pot for it belongs to Granny Willow. And I'm more frightened of her than I'll ever be of you . . . ouch!'

'Shut up, stupid,' snarled Scumm. 'The kidnapped don't pay their own ransoms.'

'That's what I said,' shouted Nettles defiantly. 'Ouch.'

'So, proud Finn!' yelled Scumm. 'Should we spare the life of your scrawny cook? And don't try sneaking down the ladder and taking us by surprise because I've posted look-outs. Try any tricks and we'll melt away into The Wilderness and you'll never see your precious Nettles again.'

'State your demands for his safe return, you vile creature!' cried Finn. 'If you want the rest of our possessions then you can have them. But be warned, torture Nettles any more and you'll plead for death when I catch up with you.'

'We stole all we wanted from you back in the cavern,' sneered Scumm. 'And a very poor haul it was. We're interested in the Forest People. It's rumoured that they are enormously rich. That they have heaps of gold and jewels hidden away that they never use. If they agree to give us a few chestfuls of it then Nettles won't have to face a gory death. So will they agree to my demands? After all, if you must make friends then what are they for, but to help out in a crisis? We Scavengers await your answer.'

'Though we lust for treasure we'd love to keep Nettles too,' said a wistful voice. 'Earlier today we forced him to cook us a stew. And what did it taste like, my fellow scavengers?'

'Like the food of the Gods,' shouted his friends, smacking their lips. 'We never knew that wild roots could taste so deliciously good.'

'But Nettles refused to give us the recipe,' said a sad voice. 'Even though I gave him a good tweaking to reveal his hidden sources.'

'And I never will!' yelled Nettles from the darkness. 'I'd rather be killed by Scumm than by Granny Willow if she found out I'd blabbed about her secret ingredients.'

'Well, you've heard my terms,' shouted Scumm. 'In return for your cook we demand as many chestfuls of treasure as we can stagger away with. And while you're about it those forest clowns can throw in a few of their fancy leaf-cloaks, for I see myself in one of those. Refuse my demands and Nettles will suffer the agony of a double-death. First the death from a thousand dagger cuts. Then afterwards he'll be smeared with honey and staked out on an ant-hill to endure the death from a thousand bites. It's called overkill, for we Scavengers never do things by halves. So, what do your cosy new friends say to that, humbled Finn? Will they give up their treasure to save this puny cook's life?'

'You blackmailing savage,' cried Pansy, shaking her fist into the darkness below. 'You and your scavenging gang are beneath contempt.'

'And proud of it!' Scumm sneered back. 'We rob for greed and kill for thrills. We don't expect our way of life to be admired. Anyway, loose-tongued girl, I'm not talking to you. We scavengers teach our women with regular beatings to keep their big mouths shut. Someone should teach you the same.'

'And you need teaching some good manners,' shouted Pansy, enraged. She had to be restrained from clambering down the ladder to do battle.

'Tell the Forest people to refuse, Finn,' yelled Nettles. 'Tell them to keep their treasure close to

186

their chests. I'll face my double-death from cuts and bites with courage. Just go on with the quest to the end of the tail and leave me to sacrifice my life for the noble cause we set out on . . . ouch!'

'I've twisted his nose this time,' warned Scumm. 'The next time I'll twist it clean off. For the last time, over-proud Finn, bow to my will or this brat dies.'

'I can't pledge the wealth of the Forest People,' shouted angry Finn. 'I can't give you things that aren't mine. Back in the cavern you swore to kill me, Scumm. Well I offer myself alone and unarmed in place of Nettles. Torture me as you will, but let that tiny boy go.'

'No, I can't allow it, my friend,' said Old Ashwold, gently patting his shoulder. 'Whatever my people have is yours to bargain with. The problem is we don't have the riches that Scumm lusts after. Such rumours have tagged us for most of our history. But how does one explain that our gold and silver and precious jewels are in the very nature of the world around us? The morning sun is golden, the riding moon our silver delight. And as for the jewels we are said to hoard, they are the stars in the sky. For our wealth has always been in our way of life. But what little we have in the form of earthly trinkets we'll gladly give to save the life of small Nettles.'

'We're getting impatient, Finn,' shouted Scumm from below. 'We're still waiting for the chests of treasure to come tumbling down. Only then will you get Nettles back, tweaked, but mostly unharmed. When we've got the treasure and made our getaway you'll find your scrawny cook tied to a tree. But your time is running out, worried Finn.'

The questers were beside themselves with grief and worry. The gathered Forest people felt much the same. For though Nettles was a nuisance he was also much missed and loved. The thought of him suffering two deaths in a row was appalling. While Finn with heavy heart was thanking Old Ashwold for his offer of trinkets that he knew would be scoffed at by Scumm, a bounding shape was flying into action on the forest floor below.

Not a soul had seen Sage slip away some time before. Now she was in among the evil Scavengers tossing them left and right with blows from her paws and her battering-ram of a nose. Dodging the dagger swipes of her enemies she fought her way to the spot where Scumm held squirming Nettles captive. As she attempted to snatch him away she was all at once overwhelmed by the gang of Scavengers who had recovered from the shock of it all. Resisting to the end, the brave watervole was beaten to the ground and tethered to a tree by a cruel twist of bramble. Now the Scavengers held captive two quest members. The triumph in Scumm's voice was sickening to hear as the weeping folk on the back of the Great Snake gazed unseeingly down into the blackness below.

'I warned you about trying to sneak down,' spat Scumm. 'Now we're also holding your pet rat prisoner. Which means we demand twice the amount of treasure you don't want to part with. So, are you going to charm your Forest friends into parting with their riches, Finn, or is their kindliness a bluff to hide their meanness?'

'You can have all we have, Scumm!' cried Old Ashwold. 'Though our treasures have never amounted to more than a few baubles and trinkets. Take them as I toss them down, but please return your captives to the bosom of their friends, I beseech you,' and he threw down the hastily collected few objects his Forest People owned. It was a small and pathetic ransom. No more than a few gold and silver personal keepsakes. But it was all the so-called treasure the Forest People owned. Everyone waited anxiously for Scumm's reaction. It came swift and loud.

'Miserly liars!' he bellowed. 'You must think us fools to be fobbed off with such junk. Where are all your heavy chests brimming with sparkling things?'

'There aren't any, there never were,' replied dignified Old Ashwold. 'We Forest People have always lived the simple life. We are rich indeed, but not in the vulgar sense you believe. Our wealth lies in this forest itself, in every leaf and blade of grass you vandals trample on.'

'So, we are treading on chests of buried treasure?' bawled Scumm greedily. 'Cunningly hidden beneath the grass? Well, throw down a map and a few sharp shovels or these two hostages will die as sure as my name is Scavenger Scumm.'

'We can't give what we don't possess,' replied Old Ashwold helplessly.

'Meaning, what you possess you won't give,' shouted Scumm angrily. 'Well, if that's the way it's going to be then we Scavengers are going to do a bit of hoarding of our own. Are you listening, failed leader Finn? You think you're good at exploring, well you can explore for the two hostages we intend to take into The Wilderness. And make sure your expedition brings lots of treasure to bargain with. Because if you don't your two precious friends will suffer a double-death each, and very slowly to drag out their agony. So, we'll meet again in The Wilderness. You won't see us, but we'll see you. Just follow the windings of the great snake and we won't be far away, ever watching.'

'And in the meantime we'll be enjoying wonderful stews,' said a happy Scavenger. 'And I'm sure that with a few warm hugs I can coax the secret recipes from him before he's ransomed or killed.'

'Come brothers, we've delayed enough,' snapped Scumm. 'Let's leave our enemies to sweat and worry and make up their minds about the ransom. And as a parting reminder that we're deadly serious we'll persuade our prisoners to make their last appeals to the misers on the back of the snake who love treasure more than their friends. First a few words from the small cook.'

'Ouch!' yelled Nettles. 'Can't you find a less

tender spot to tweak, you brute. But I can take it, Finn. I'm determined to hold out until you and the questers come and rescue me and brave Sage. And while we're waiting for rescue, me and Sage will be trying to escape by digging tunnels underneath our prison. Scumm and his gang will soon learn that they can't hold Sage, daughter of Sedge, and Nettles, a warrior of the Willow clan, for long. And when everything is over and the battle against evil has been won I'll be expecting a medal for bravery when I get home to our valley. Presented by Granny Willow, of course. Ouch!'

'So much for the cook's wishful thinking, Finn,' taunted Scumm. 'Now let's hear a few words from the water-rat who seems strangely quiet tethered to her tree. Perhaps a small prod from my dagger will loosen her tongue . . .'

Sage's sharp cry of pain was heartrending. The hearts of the listeners above seethed with both compassion and anger. But there was nothing they could do to help their captured friends. Her voice, though distressed, drifted up loud and clear.

'Finn, fellow questers, if I die then be sure that I died defending Nettles first and myself second. This is no bravery. As the daughter of my honourable father I could do nothing else. Just give him my love and tell him I did my duty.'

'One last chance,' yelled Scumm. 'Are you going to hand over your treasure or not? I think you should know the depths of evil I'm prepared to sink to. I'd kill my own grandmother for a chestful of treasure. I'd sacrifice all of my craven followers if it would make me personally richer. That's what kind of Scavenger I am, that's why I'm a much-feared leader.'

'And he is too,' agreed his nervous gang. 'Even though Scumm means everything to us, we mean nothing to him at all. That's the kind of Scavengers we are. We're always cowered in his presence, and so it should be.'

'Now you know the situation,' called Scumm, harshly.

'And you already know our situation,' cried Old Ashwold. 'We have nothing to give, if only we had, you could have it.'

'Brag and boast and bully as you will, Scumm,' Finn's deadly serious voice sounded down into the darkness. 'But I promise you'll weep for the arms of your grandmother if you harm one hair on the heads of my friends.'

'Oh, enough of this noble guff,' snarled Scumm, impatiently. 'You know our terms. You'll find us in The Wilderness which is our homeland, if you wish to make a deal. You'll sense us in the drifting fogs that swirl around our birthplace. You'll hear us on the winds that moan along the sides of the Great Golden Snake. You hate us as we hate you, pathetic Finn. All the People have histories, and we have histories too. I read my books as you did yours. And they told me much about the Land of The People we all inhabit. In the ancient words we were warned . . . go empty-handed and come back empty-hearted . . . if there's right to be done get

195

your wrong in first so the right can't be wrong to you . . . many wisdoms like that are contained in our clan histories, and we obey them to the last puzzling letter. For we all believe what we're raised to believe, and are blind to everything else.'

'I believe your histories are harsh and wrong,' wept Pansy. 'Look into your soul and into the eyes of your captives, Scumm. Let our people go.'

'Talking about going,' said Scumm in a loud voice. He was ignoring her and addressing his gang. 'Tether our hostages so they can't escape, and let's away. Draw your cowls over your faces as we hurry through the trees to our next secret hiding-place. We want no twittering of terrified birds to betray the route we take back to our wilderness home. Quick now, let's scurry back into the shadows before the cursed sun rises . . .' There then drifted up to the back of the great snake the sounds of snapping twigs and thrashing ferns, then silence.

Shock reigned for long moments after the swift departure of the Scavengers. What words could describe the heartless and brutal things that had happened so suddenly to a small brave cook and a water-vole, snatched so quickly away from the protection of the questers.

'How does one reason against such blind hatred?' said Old Ashwold, hopelessly. 'I fear for the safety of your friends, Finn. If only we Forest People could help more. What will you do now, dear friend?'

'We will continue the quest, but now with twin aims,' said Finn, grimly. 'Firstly to rescue Nettles and Sage from the clutches of those demon Scavengers, then next to free the end of the snake's tail from those equally mad Doomsday People. Those are my aims, Old Ashwold. We questers knew the dangers we faced when we first set out. We took on and defeated some. Doubtless we'll meet with more. But only cowards turn back from the goals they set when the heartaches and dangers mount.'

'Order us to turn back and we'd refuse, Finn,' cried the questers gathered around him and Old Ashwold. 'This expedition is determined to rescue Nettles and Sage from the clutches of the Scavengers, and then to travel on to the end of the tail.'

'Then I can only wish you well with all of my heart,' said sad Old Ashwold. 'And hope that you succeed in your ventures, to afterwards return safe home to your loved ones. And from a selfish point of view may your triumphs allow our Great Snake to at last curl up with his tail for a well-deserved sleep. He's suffered enough these past one thousand years, God bless him.'

'We'll do our best, I promise,' vowed Finn. 'After we've slept away some of our own tiredness.'

'Forgive me,' apologised Old Ashwold. 'I'm keeping you all from your beds, and you with so much to do in the morning. Tomorrow my people will accompany you along the snake's back to the farther edge of our forest. But that's as far as they dare go, Finn. For beyond lies The Wilderness that our histories have banned us from entering. We only know that some of our Guardian cousins live there in order to tend our Great Snake. And as we both know, its also the haunt of those terrible Scavengers who enjoy to destroy the lives of peaceful folk. I wish you didn't have to enter that terrible place, Finn, but I know you're determined to. I wish I was young and strong again. I wish I had rebelled against the fears written into our history books. I wish I'd have been an adventurer in my youth as you are, Finn. But now I'm old and still afraid of the mysteries that surround The Wilderness with all its taboos for us Forest folk. Perhaps one day my daughter Scarlet and her friends will break the spell of our sacred books and stride out to see for themselves the whole of the land of the People. But for me with a mind so set in the past, such freedoms are not for me. How I yearn to be young and marching by your side, Finn. But it will always be a dream for me.'

'You'll be with us in spirit, Old Ashwold,' said Finn, patting the oldster's bowed shoulders. 'We'll always feel your calm and guiding presence even though we'll never meet again. But let the future lie in tomorrow's fate, and hope that the new day dawns with a lucky sun smiling on we questers.'

'Then I bid you all goodnight,' said Old Ashwold, deeply moved. 'Farewell, and good travelling in the morning. I won't be awake to see you off, my aching bones you know. When youth fades to memory it takes all nimbleness too, young Finn.'

'Goodnight and thanks, old friend,' said Finn, embracing him. 'No matter what happens tomorrow, we'll never forget the kindness of you Forest People.'

Everyone began to drift away to the huts and bed. Angered and deeply grieved by the brutal kidnapping of Nettles and Sage, the questers sensibly knew that they would need all the sleep they could get to be in a fit state to rescue their dear ones. They would also need all the alertness they could muster to tackle the mysterious Wilderness where their friends were being held captive. Sometimes fitful, sometimes deep, sleep wove its magic till morning.

The magpie was perched on the low eave of one of the huts, also trying to sleep. But his misery kept waking him up. He felt so useless with one pain-filled wing out of action. How could he scout the dangerous Wilderness ahead being crippled so? He was supposed to be the scouting eyes of his friends in times of danger. Yet at this time he could barely flap more than a short distance along the golden back of the Great Snake. He hated to think he was letting his friends down even though he had received his injuries during the battle with the spiders. He knew his flying skills might be desperately needed when the expedition entered the mysterious unknown of Scavenger domain, The Wilderness. The young magpie tried to cheer himself up. Perhaps his wing would be better by morning. Perhaps the healing cure of sleep would do the trick. He shifted his claws on the eave and flexed his troublesome wing. Wincing with pain, he tenderly tucked it away. Closing his beady eyes he willed for sleep to come. Then he remembered an old remedy for insomnia his father had taught him. Thinking hard he imagined himself in the middle of a green meadow that was strewn with glittering objects of great worth and beauty. In his greed to gather them all and fly back to his nest, his snatching beak grasped one jewel, only to drop another. And so it went on, the futile attempt to have everything only to end up with nothing. The chick bird never got around to the solution, which was 'one thing at a time', for he was already fast asleep.

Lying once more on his soft leafy bed Finn gazed up at his comfort, the night sky. As his eyes scanned the familiar star patterns, he was saddened by what he saw. The comet that the Great Snake had pinned his hopes on was streaking away from earth and back into the depths of space. The bright friend of the unsleeping creature had had no advice to offer that lonely one. Equally lonely itself, the comet having rounded the world was off on another deep and wandering journey to meet with a destiny of its own. And suddenly Finn felt lonely and afraid himself. He had eagerly accepted the role of leader back in the great oak. Yet under that leadership the expedition had lost two dead and many wounded. Now the grieving questers had to come to terms with the snatching away of Nettles and loyal Sage. Tomorrow the expedition would enter The Wilderness where their friends were being held captive by the Scavengers. And if their rescue wasn't dangerous enough there was still the trek to the end of the tail to be completed, to free the tail from the mysterious Doomsday clan. Half awake and half asleep the fisher-boy tossed and turned and muttered his doubts to himself.

'Your first expedition ended in shipwreck and

humiliation, stupid Finn. You've been offered another chance to prove that you are a great explorer. Will you lead this quest into disaster also? How many trusting lives must be lost in this second attempt to prove yourself? Turn back, foolish boy, turn back . . . but what of Nettles and Sage in danger of their lives and praying for us to rescue them?'

Once more he felt a silent presence beside him, felt a coolness mopping his fevered brow.

'Sleep away the horrors of this day, Finn,' said Scarlet softly. 'And wake refreshed when the sun comes up, for tomorrow is another day.'

Eleven

THE DOOMSDAY CLAN

During the trek through the meadowlands, Stroller had listened closely as Finn had spoken of the oak in the valley and the Willow clan who lived there. Proudly the boy had said he was an adopted son of that family since sailing away from his fisher-folk people in search of adventure. Stroller had also listened intently while Umber had described his life as a Guardian back home in the cave of tears. How he and his clan had for centuries lovingly tended the trapped head of the Great Golden Snake. Stroller, being the cunning spy he was, already knew this. But he was surprised to learn that the Guardians of the cave were rather timid people. Not at all the fierce folk who defended the snake with their lives as written in the Doomsday histories. As he slyly milked them of information an idea began to form in Stroller's fertile mind. His clan had always avoided an assault on the snake's head for fear of the vicious Guardians who protected him. That was the reason they had always attacked his more vulnerable tail. They had long ago captured and pinned it down in a secret place. The hope was that the head would die from pining. But it hadn't, and so a stalemate had existed between the Guardian and the Doomsday clans. One clan claimed the head, the other the tail, and never the twain would meet. But now that ancient stand-off seemed such a fearful waste of time to Stroller's present thinking, as he sauntered through the meadowlands between the trusting Finn and Umber. He felt very angry that in the past not one leader of his clan had suggested a frontal attack to destroy the Great Golden Snake when all the while his feeble Guardians had been there for the taking. It was just before he led the band of innocents into the prepared spider-trap when the solution struck him. How did one destroy once and for all a snake that threatened the whole of one's world? The answer was startlingly simple. To the surprise of Finn and Umber he suddenly stopped in mid-stride.

'Of course, you fool,' he exclaimed aloud to himself. 'Destroy the head and the tail will wither.'

'What was that, Stroller?' said Finn, alarmed.

'Oh, just a private thought, just something about nothing,' smiled Stroller, walking on. 'I often talk to myself, my life being so solitary. But before we reach our journey's end, could you tell me more about this Robin and his Fern who rule your valley home?'

'Oh no, they don't rule, Stroller,' Finn hastened to explain. 'They're much too kind and fair-minded for that. Though they can be firm, they see their roles as the advisors of the Willow clan.'

'Kind and fair-minded, eh?' mused Stroller, smiling his extra-wide smile. 'I'll look forward to meeting them some day soon. In fact, as soon as possible.'

'My people in the cave of tears would also love to meet you, Stroller,' said Umber shyly. 'If you could spare the time from your wanderings, that is. They rarely get to meet interesting visitors from the world outside.'

'I think a meeting can be arranged,' replied Stroller warmly. But his eyes remained as cold as ice.

And there the conversation ended. They were now approaching the old rabbit tunnel shortcut that dived under the snake's belly. Despite the evil joy he felt, Stroller managed to stay calm. For he needed to keep the trust of the nervous questers in order to do the dirty deed he had planned for them. But inside he was itching to be away on his next and final mission to destroy the Great Golden Snake once and for all. At the entrance to the tunnel with the smiling Black Spider looking on he had drawn aside the thick web and motioned to the friends to follow him inside, smiling all the while. And while smiling, whispering jubilant words to himself: 'Be calm my heart, our battles will be won . . . but first of all let's stir this stew till done . . .'

He wasn't strolling now but hurrying, his mind awhirl with plans. No longer was he the simple wanderer but the Lord Stroller in his true and wicked colours. He had been the leader of the Doomsday clan since the death of his beloved father. He vividly remembered his old father lying on his death-bed clutching at his hand and gasping his last words.

'Every Doomsday clan leader has failed to destroy our enemy the Great Golden Snake, my son. I beseech you, succeed where others have failed for the sake of our people. I have faith in you, my son. Finish the task that I couldn't . . .' and then he had died with one huge, regretful sigh.

The new Lord Stroller hurried on, determined to triumph where his father had failed. With every fibre of his being he yearned to be the one to bring the Great Snake's life to a painful and final end. For brief moments he stopped and turned and craned his ears to listen. Were those screams on the night air the sound of the questers going to their deaths? Convinced that they were, Stroller chuckled and hurried on. Now he was travelling back through the meadowlands, the moonlit bulk of the snake his guide. Soon he was standing on the grassy knoll where he had cunningly made friends with the questers only that morning. That same spot where he had cynically shared their breakfast and goodwill. For a while he stood on the knoll peering into the shadows that danced in the moonlight, his mane of black hair and his sweeping cloak fluttering in the breeze. Then he tensed as he heard a challenge from not too far away.

'Have you a name, shadow on the hill?' it demanded. 'Is it the name of a leader who's been two long days gone? Give us that name in a tone we recognise. Name correctly and you'll enjoy your favourite supper of roast nightingales tonight. Name the wrong name and we'll creep up there and slit your throat for an impostor.'

Cupping his hands around his mouth, the shadowy figure on the grassy knoll replied, 'It is I . . . your Lord Stroller. Come and attend me.'

'Impostors often steal the names of people high above them,' said the voice suspiciously. 'Can you prove you are Lord Stroller, the leader we fear and adore? Don't move a muscle unless you wish to be crucified upon the nearest tree.'

'I'm your leader in person,' snapped Stroller,

getting irritated. 'I admire your caution but don't overdo it. I'm coming down to join you.'

'And if you aren't who you say you are, you'll pay with your life for saying who you aren't,' warned the voice firmly. 'Saying things that aren't true is the same as telling a lie. And I hate liars who stand on grassy knolls pretending to be someone else. If you are the leader we hope you are, then you'd better hope you are.'

'And I advise you to shut up,' snapped their Lord Stroller, patience gone and storming down the hill. 'Now do you know me?'

'Yes, Lord Stroller,' said the look-out, timidly emerging from a bramble-bush. 'I was trying to be good at my job.'

'And good you were,' said Stroller, calming down. 'Just don't try to be so good in future. And now, where are our other brothers?'

The relieved look-out turned and uttered a secret owl-hoot that was a mystery to the birds themselves who stared down from their perches with never a blink. At once the surrounding nettle-beds and turfy clumps began to part. Soon figures were emerging from their hides, their delight plain on their smiling faces. Quickly they gathered around Stroller, questions babbling from their lips.

'What news, great leader?' they asked anxiously. 'Has the trap been sprung on the travellers? Or do they still march along the great snake on their quest to free his tail from our clutches?'

'Their marching days are over,' smiled Stroller viciously. 'Our Black Spider friends have dealt with them in the usual way. Those who feel pity for the snake can expect no mercy from us. Why, my brothers?'

'Because it's written in our histories,' someone cried. 'That should the head and the tail ever meet they'll crush the life from the lands of the People. Then earthquakes will shudder and fire will ravage the foundations of our way of life. And we'll be forced to flee into The Wilderness to live the bestial lives of Scumm and the dirty Scavengers.'

'Thus mightily will the Doomsday People suffer,' said the look-out gravely. 'My dad told me that.'

'Soon all our fears will belong to the past,' said Stroller, his cold eyes sparkling in the moonlight. 'For I've thought of a plan to destroy the Great Golden Snake once and for all.'

'This calls for a celebration!' cried someone. 'Let's hurry back to our secret place and honour Lord Stroller with feasting and the supping of dandelion wine. Our leader must be starving for his favourite supper of roast nightingales after the dirty deed he was forced to do for our clan. Afterwards he can tell us about his brilliant plan.'

'I wish I had brilliant ideas and plans,' said the envious look-out. 'I hope our Lord Stroller finds a role for me in his plan to wipe out the Great Snake. I hope he won't hold it against me because I threatened to slit his throat. I was only following orders and doing my duty, after all. I'd love to embrace him but he'd probably think I was hiding my dagger behind my back.'

'You did your duty, small, sly one,' said Stroller, patting his cringing shoulders. 'But now, let's away to our secret place and relax awhile. We've lots to talk about in the hours still left till dawn . . .' and in single file he led his followers off to the place that only the Doomsday clan knew about. After many twists and turns along a cunning maze of paths they finally arrived.

Inside the trunk of a hollow tree a fire was burning. Roasting and spitting over the flames were a dozen or so plucked nightingales wafting delicious smells around the cramped confines. Soon Stroller and his followers were hungrily tucking in. The folk of the Doomsday clan had always believed that nightingales tasted much better than they sang.

The hollow tree grew deep in the woods overlooking the valley of the Willow clan. The

crude dwelling was just one of the many out-
posts strung around the circle of the Great
Golden Snake. These secret hides were used
as the eyes and the ears of the Doomsday clan
who spied on everyone travelling along the
snake with purpose unknown. Only the slinking
Scavengers were ignored and allowed free
passage to pursue their sordid way of life. But
total strangers were something else. It was rare
to see such people travelling along the snake.
They always aroused deep suspicion among the
Doomsday watchers. Why would strangers trek
along the coils of the Great Golden Snake if not
to arrive at the end of the tail? And what would
they find if allowed to arrive there? That was the
disturbing question for the secretive Doomsday
clan. For if permitted to journey on the strangers
would discover in a concealed and sacred place
the tail of the Great Snake pinioned and staked
to the ground by a thousand stout vines. The
Doomsday clan were merciless in their means to
prevent such a meeting. It spelled death for all

inquisitive strangers who sought to pry into the secrets of their age-old obsession. And so Finn and his hopeful friends had died in the lair of the Black Spiders, as had many questers before them. Yet, though the Lord Stroller sitting by the fire in the hollow tree had reason to be pleased with himself for the dirty deed he had recently done, he still had problems to sort out. His plan to destroy the Great Snake once and for all meant that other enemies had to be disposed of. Namely, the Robin and Fern he had heard so much about, plus the Guardian nuisances who fussily tended the head of the snake in the cave of tears. But he was confident that when the time came he would despatch them as easily as he had the stupid Finn and his pathetic rabble.

As had all creatures and peoples of the earth, the Doomsday clan had watched the rising and the setting of the sun since the beginning of time. But that clan so burdened with doom saw no beauty in those sights, but merely the passing of days and nights. Neither could the changing seasons quicken their stony hearts. They hated the winter for its snow that made them shiver. They disliked the spring because the happy birds sang much too loudly and merrily. They detested the hot summer for its laziness. As for the autumn, its bright flowers and orange leaves were too gaudy for their taste. The only pleasure the Doomsday clan enjoyed was the passing of those seasons that ticked away another year from the life of their ancient enemy. Only when he was dead would they be truly happy. The clan yearned for the day when the Great Golden Snake lay slumped in lifeless coils around the lands of the People, his destructive circle uncompleted. At last, the late feast of juicy nightingales washed down with dandelion wine was over. After the last bone had been gnawed, when greasy mouths had been wiped on the sleeves of tunics, Lord Stroller rose from his place beside the fire and began to speak.

'And now to my plan,' he began, gazing

around at the worshipping faces. 'It can be summed up in a few simple words. Destroy the head and the tail will wither . . .'

'Whither to where?' interrupted the puzzled look-out. 'I can't see it wandering far the way we've got it tied down. If the head of the snake was destroyed the tail would be too distressed to do much whithering and pithering and zithering every which way.'

'I meant that the tail would die without the head,' snapped Stroller. 'My plan is that we attack and kill the snake's head in the cave of tears. Once that is achieved the tail will expire from natural causes. Our clan should have done this countless years ago, but lacked the genius to think of it. It has been passed on to me, your present Lord Stroller, to solve the problem that has plagued our clan since time began. We inside this hollow tree will be forever remembered in our histories as the ones who slew the Great Golden Snake and saved the world from his vengeful destruction.'

'What about the Guardians who protect the snake so fiercely?' asked a fearful follower. 'We've always been warned that they pounce on all strangers who venture near their cave and gobble their hearts and livers for breakfast.'

'Those old stories are myth,' scoffed Stroller. 'I've met and spoken with a Guardian from the cave of the snake and he was a soft and pathetic creature. He and his clan are shrinking violets when it comes to violence. As for gobbling down their enemies, they live on a bland diet of fish stew and sickly honey. I can assure you all, they'll be no trouble to us when we enter their cave and destroy the head of the snake. But there is a "but".'

'I thought there'd be a "but",' said the disappointed look-out. 'I was all fired up to dash off and tackle the cave Guardians single-handed. Now your ominous "but" has ruined my plan. You've knocked all the bluster from my sails, Lord Stroller. You talk just like our history books. They also pepper good news with depressing "buts".'

'I have good reason to be cautious,' snapped Stroller. 'During the walk through the meadow-lands I also quizzed the leader of the expedition. His name is Finn, or it was Finn before he met his end in the lair of the Black Spiders. He spoke with great respect and feeling about a certain Robin and Fern who protect the Willow clan in the valley below. Finn said that the pair were kind and fair-minded. Yet he also said that they were seasoned adventurers and warriors who wouldn't hesitate to kill anyone who threatened their people. Now, I ask you, how can folk be kind and fair-minded and ruthless killers all at the same time? So I've decided that before we tackle the cave of the Guardians we must lull and charm away the suspicions of this Robin and his Fern. Then we'll wait for the right moment to strike them down, thus clearing our way to the head of the snake. My plan is that we employ our greatest skill. That of disguise which we Doomsday people have always been masters of. For it's clear we couldn't take on the might of the Willow clan in a full-frontal attack, we being so few at this time.'

'We few, we precious few,' nodded the look-out, wiping away a tear. 'We band of brothers who stick together through thick and thin.'

'There's little time left till dawn,' said Stroller, urgently. 'We must completely transform our appearances before we stroll down into the valley of the Willow clan and introduce our-selves to Robin and his Fern. I suggest we become a small and pious band of Great Snake worshippers, come to bow before our reptile God. Are we all agreed on that?'

'We are, Lord Stroller!' shouted his followers.

'I love dressing-up,' said the look-out gleefully. 'I always feel happier being someone else than myself.'

'But more important than disguise is the method we need to kill the snake,' said Lord Stroller thoughtfully. 'Once we've tricked our way into the cave, how do we destroy that cursed head? It's too huge and thick-skinned

222

to hack to death with our weapons. Some cunning method is needed.'

'I think I have the answer,' said a soft voice from beside the flickering fire. The speaker rose to address them all. Like all of the Doomsday people he wore a long black cloak close-wrapped around him. Unlike them he wore atop his straggly dark hair a small skullcap made from the black and yellow skins of vicious stinging wasps. The followers shuddered for they knew him well. He was the one who yanked out their aching teeth and plied them with bitter medicines when they felt out of sorts. He was the one usually to be found cutting up insects and tiny animals and muttering over their remains. When the Doomsday folk did feel well they avoided him and his noxious smells like the plague. In short, he was a necessary evil in the lives of his people. He rarely spoke, so he had the full attention of his cross-legged audience as he continued.

'As you know, my father was a master of potions and taught me all his skills before he died. Long ago he whispered to me of a poison so deadly that a single drop could wipe out the whole of the People. I believe that a few drops more would kill our giant enemy stone dead. I know where the poison can be found, but how could we get the Great Snake to swallow it? It's so bitter he'd immediately suspect and spit it out in disgust.'

'Honey is my answer to that,' shouted the look-out, shocking his friends with his sudden brilliance. 'If we mixed the deadly poison with a dollop of sweet honey its evil would be masked by sweetness.'

'An inspired idea,' said Lord Stroller, impressed. He patted the pleased and blushing look-out. 'Prepare to be promoted in the near future, lowly one.'

'What poison could have such power?' questioned someone. 'That just a few drops could kill the Great Golden Snake who dwarfs our lands?'

'There is a stagnant pool not far from here,'

smiled the master of potions. 'And on its lily-pad squats a tiny orange toad with emerald eyes. He spends his life weeping and gulping down gnats and croaking his loneliness through the night, for he longs for a wife. When disturbed by strangers he attacks in fury. His weapon is his spitting power that spews forth gobs of venom that result in instant death for all those who dare to invade his space. So, Lord Stroller, to kill the great snake we need to collect the spit of the tiny orange toad. Blended with extra sweet honey it should be quite tasteless. I'm sure the snake would eagerly swallow our bait.'

'Now my great plan is coming together,' said Stroller, delighted. 'Sneak into the night and collect your poison, master of potions. In the meantime, others will be out stealing the richest of honey from the dreaming bees.'

'Of course, I'll need an assistant,' said the medicine man. 'I'll need someone to poke the toad with a stick, to goad him into a fury while I hold the bowl to catch the spit.'

'Why are you looking at me?' cried the frightened look-out. 'It's promotion I want, not certain death if the toad spits in my face. And I've always hated slimy toads with bulging eyes.'

'That's your promotion, take it or leave it,' said Stroller impatiently. 'Off you go with your master. And if the orange toad should spit straight in your eye just remember that you're dying for the sake of our Doomsday clan.'

'I wish to state that I'm being promoted under pressure,' were the look-out's bitter remarks as he followed the master of potions from the hollow tree. 'And I'd much rather keep my humble job of peering through bushes . . .'

'And now to think of a suitable disguise,' mused Lord Stroller, glancing around at the eager faces of his followers. 'In the morning we must appear to Robin and Fern of the Willow clan as pious and humble worshippers of the Great Golden Snake, come bearing gifts of special honey. Your jobs will simply be to look the part of awed and gentle pilgrims come to bow before The Great One. Don't speak, just smile and look saintly. The necessary weasel words just leave to me. But back to the subject of our cunning disguise, my followers. What do we always do if we need to look kind and innocent?'

'We turn our coats,' chorused the circle around the fire.

'And that is what we're going to do,' said Stroller, grinning evilly. With a swift movement he took the Black Spider wig from his head and turned it inside-out. Then he clapped it back on. The transformed wig was suddenly a tumble of golden curls and looked very angelic indeed. Then he shrugged from his cloak and turned that too. Now it hung to the floor in beautiful silver folds. Soon all the followers were apeing him, giggling among themselves as they posed and preened in their new attire. Now in the firelight they resembled a cluster of cherubs, all trace of their dark garb hidden from view. Where once had been evil, now goodness reigned. Or appeared to. For the true souls of the Doomsday clan nestled close and black about them. And the gold and silver of their new outward appearances was false and dross, easily exposed if tomorrow some curious one reached out to scratch away that surface brightness . . .

'Is everything prepared?' snapped Lord Stroller, just before dawn.

'Everything,' his followers assured him. 'The poison, the honey, our widest and kindest smiles, all are prepared, Lord Stroller.'

'Let us then waste no more time,' said Stroller, adjusting his golden wig and his silver cloak. 'We need to be down in the valley of the Willow clan before sunrise, there to begin our busy work.'

It was a beautiful sight to see, the Doomsday people filing from the hollow tree in that pre-dawn moment. Clad in the colours of goodness, their white smiles bright, they looked like saintly wraiths in motion as they followed their

Lord Stroller along the paths through the wood and down into the valley of the Willow clan. But their eyes, their hard and cruel eyes were cold . . .

Twelve

PILGRIMS BEARING GIFTS

'Robin . . . Robin . . .' hissed an urgent voice. A hand shook the leader awake. 'I was out picking mushrooms and guess what?'

'Who are you, waking me up to babble about mushrooms?' grumbled Robin, turning over in his warm bed. 'Can't it wait until the sun rises?'

'It's me, Fern,' the voice persisted. 'You know

I wouldn't wake you just to talk about mushrooms. This is important. While a group of us were out picking mushrooms for Granny Willow we were startled by strangers who asked to be taken to our leader. I think you should get out of bed, Robin, for you're needed at the foot of our tree, immediately.'

'Oh, very well,' sighed Robin, crawling from his birds-down quilt. 'Am I allowed the time to stretch and yawn and dress? I'm sure the world won't end while I'm pulling on my breeches. Go down and tell the strangers that I'm on my way.'

'Yes, Robin,' said Fern, hurrying off. 'And make an effort to look tidy for our pretty visitors.'

'Pretty?' mused Robin to himself, as he stretched and yawned and dressed. A short while later he was climbing down through the branches of the oak to find out what the fuss was all about. Reaching the grassy floor below, he was shocked to be suddenly surrounded by a crush of Willow folk all babbling at the tops of their voices and pointing towards a small clearing among the trees. Rubbing the sleep from his eyes, Robin looked. Then he rubbed and stared again. A look of astonishment appeared on his face as he gazed at the sight confronting his eyes.

Standing serenely in the clearing was a group of the most beautiful people he had ever seen. Their long golden hair glowed in the rays of the rising sun. They wore long silver cloaks that swept the grass and the flowers they stood upon. Their eyes could not be seen for their heads were humbly downcast. But there was no mistaking their noses. All of the strangers had noses both upturned and broad that told relieved Robin that they weren't angels from heaven, but firmly of the People. So it was with curiosity rather than fear that Robin with Fern at his side approached the strangers. As they did so one of the visitors moved forward to meet them. He was a leader himself, no doubt about that. Though his blonde head was bowed there was an air of authority about him. As the two leaders came within touching distance the stranger raised his head and smiled. It was a smile so warm and gentle that Robin's wariness melted away. For a while Robin was at a loss for words and could only stare. Though dressed in his best tunic and hose he felt like a humble peasant in the presence of the finely dressed visitor. He began to fumble for words and was grateful when Fern nudged him in the ribs and murmured in his ear.

'All that glitters is not gold, Robin,' she whispered. 'Be proud and take strength from the pride the Willow people feel for you. Politely introduce yourself, then ask the stranger who he is, and what he wants.'

'I'm Robin, leader of the Willow clan,' said Robin, finding his voice. He held out his hand which was warmly clasped by the other. 'Please declare yourself, stranger, and tell me what we can do for you.'

'My name is Brother Pilgrim,' replied the

stranger, bowing. 'My followers and I have journeyed for many moons along the length of the Great Golden Snake to reach this valley, our destination. We have come to worship the head of the Great Snake in his cave of tears. For since the world began, his bulk has been a protecting wall around the lands of the People. We have come to show our gratitude. My Pilgrim clan has long yearned to visit the shrine where his head lies trapped, to pay him homage. Our ancient histories predicted that one day a mighty comet would flash across the heavens, and that we pilgrims would follow its path around the world until it paused above a sacred place before streaking away for ever. This valley is that sacred place, and here we are to worship our hero. We just want to gaze into his wondrous face and offer him a small but precious gift as a token of our love. Bring forward the gift, novice pilgrim.'

It was the cue for a very small pilgrim to hurry forward carrying a finely-carved chest bound with gold. Such was the Willow clan's fascination with these beautiful pilgrims that they paid little attention to the puffing carrier of the heavy chest. Had they looked close they would have noticed that there was little of the pious pilgrim about him. His eyes were darting shiftily around at the surrounding bushes. His nervousness would have suggested that he longed to be in the centre of a bush, peering out at this scene from the safety there. At that point Brother Pilgrim moved to whisper a few smiling words into the small one's ear. The novice's shaking instantly stopped.

'This gift is but a small token of our love for the Great Snake,' said Pilgrim, his bottom lip trembling with emotion as he spoke. 'It's the rarest delicacy we could find in the lands of the People. A comb of precious honey from the hive of the dreaming bees. It is said to have magical properties in its subtle blend and taste. We offer it in all humbleness to the snake we've come so far to bow before. It is the wish of we pilgrims that we can gaze into his eyes as he swallows it down. That sight will be the reward our clan have long wished for after all the centuries that the snake has dominated our sleeping and waking thoughts. All we wish is that you, Robin of the Willow clan, will help us deliver our love and our gift to the one we worship above all things. We wait for a kind reply, noble Robin.'

'I'm sure the Great Snake will be delighted with your gift, Brother Pilgrim,' said Robin, graciously. 'But you must be tired and hungry after your long journey following the tail of the comet. Welcome to the valley of the Willow clan. When you and your friends have recovered from your ordeal, I myself will guide you to the cave of tears and introduce you to the sacred snake and his Guardians. Though I'm sure you'll be able to praise and worship him when you are rested and fit again.'

'Before you get carried away there are vital questions to be asked, Robin,' whispered Fern in his ear. 'Ask Pilgrim which way they travelled along the snake. Perhaps he saw Finn and the questers passing the other way. Remember, we've heard nothing from them since they first set off. The magpie chick promised to fly back to the valley and bring us news of their progress, but he hasn't yet. So what could have happened to them?'

'I heard Fern's anxious words,' said Pilgrim, his lovely smile now sad. 'We did indeed pass your people far back along the way. They were marching into The Wilderness as we were stumbling from it. Though we were close to death we croaked a warning, begging them not to enter that terrible place. I recall their leader shouting back that he and his friends would struggle on to find the end of the tail, even if they all died in the attempt. Then they marched singing on their way, our parties passing like ships in the night, we to the head, they to heaven knows where.'

'What is this place, The Wilderness?' cried

Robin, alarmed. He was having to shout to make himself heard above the weeping and wailing of the Willow folk who were thinking the worst.

'It is a place where the sun never shines,' answered Pilgrim grimly. 'And neither does the moon at night. For there is no day and night in The Wilderness. It is a place of eternal mists and gloom. No birds fly through its leaden skies where there's never a chink of blue. Of small creatures, only moles and worms sniff and burrow through its black clay, blind to the beauty denied them from birth. Of the People, only a handful of Guardians live there, loyal and barely surviving. And of course the vicious Scavenger clan whose squalid home it is. They love to return to its stinking bogs after robbing and killing sprees. That is The Wilderness, Robin, loved only by the Scavengers who thrive in gloom and filth.'

'But you and your pilgrim brothers made it through The Wilderness,' cried Fern, snatching at hope. 'Perhaps our brave ones also did while travelling the opposite way. I refuse to believe that coming is safer than going.'

'Ah, but we had our purity of soul to help us through The Wilderness,' sighed Pilgrim, bowing his head again. 'We had our love of the Great Golden Snake to guide us into this beautiful valley where his head lies cruelly trapped in the cave of tears. I hate to ask at this sad time for you and your clan, but did your questing youngsters set out with a firm faith that would see them through the bad times?'

'They had faith in each other,' shouted a grieving lady from the crush of Willow folk, many weeping. 'They also had faith in the rightness of their cause to free the snake's tail from the evil bondage of the Doomsday clan. Isn't that faith enough?'

For a brief moment the cold eyes of Pilgrim could be glimpsed through his curtain of golden hair. They were glowing with a mirthless glee that passed unnoticed by the warm-hearted Willow folk.

'I hope with all my heart that their faith will see them through,' he replied, his voice and his sad smile oozing sympathy. 'I pray that your brave band has somehow managed to avoid the Scavengers who kill first and ask no questions later. We Pilgrims only just slipped by them, thanks to a sudden storm that distracted their attention. For though we also had faith to guide us through we had luck on our side as well. We can only hope that your dear questers have faith in their luck, and luck in their faith. For storms are fickle, and only rage and darken the skies when it suits them. It is not in their normal nature to take the side of good against evil. Now I think is the moment for all of us in this clearing to declare our faith in the safety of the lost questers. But even if they've perished in The Wilderness we can still praise their memories for trying to defeat the impossible.'

And Brother Pilgrim knelt down on the bright green grass, his followers taking his cue. Grieving and hoping against slender hope, the

Willow folk also sank to their knees. It was a cruel deception of a gentle people by a master of such deceits. The Lord Stroller, now in the guise of humble pilgrim cynically bent the Willow folk to his will. He was quite sure that the questers had gone to their deaths in the tunnel of his friends the Black Spiders. But to admit such knowledge to the Willow people might raise questions. Awkward questions that he was in no mood to answer at this heady time when he felt gloriously on the brink of destroying the Great Snake once and for all. Was he clever, cleverer than his worshipped father, the new Lord Stroller of the Doomsday clan, now kneeling humbly on the ground surrounded by a host of simple fools so easily taken in? He was, and quite soon everyone in the land of the People would know it too. Somehow he managed to keep his triumph under control as he gazed piously at the sky, his hands clasped, his smiling lips mouthing words of praise and hope for folk he cared not a jot for.

Some time before, Sedge, curled up in his water-lapped burrow across the stream, had been roused from sleep by the hubbub and wailing of his Willow friends. Alarmed, he had coaxed his old muscles and bones from bed to plunge into the racing currents to swiftly glide across and find out what the fuss was all about. At about the same time the old magpie peered over the edge of his nest and also decided to investigate. An astonishing sight had met their eyes. The small knot of golden-haired, silver-robed people, the shock and anguish of their jostling oak tree friends, plus now the mass kneeling on the grass of the congregation praying for just a tiny pinch of luck that would bring their loved ones home to them. Sedge gently nudged Fern who rose from her knees, her eyes red from weeping.

'My daughter Sage, lost in this wilderness too?' he asked, sadly.

'My chick, the pride of my life,' said the

magpie brokenly. 'Of all my treasures, he was the most precious jewel in my nest.'

'There's still hope, dear friends,' wept Fern, clutching feathers and fur as she embraced them. 'The Pilgrims survived The Wilderness, perhaps our questers will too. We can only hope and pray that they do.'

'Yet if the expedition was in desperate danger, why hasn't my son flown back to bring us word?' said the magpie, puzzled. 'He made a promise that he'd keep us informed of their progress.'

'And the courage of my daughter Sage is not for turning,' said stubborn Sedge. 'She would fight the whole world in defence of her friends. Something is not quite right about these pretty, pious pilgrims and their story.'

He was just about to voice more suspicions when Robin rose from his knees to speak to his distraught Willow family. He was joined by Brother Pilgrim who stood at his side, his golden head humbly bowed.

'We must stay calm and keep hoping,' urged Robin. 'We have no proof that our loved ones perished in The Wilderness. Brother Pilgrim only said they might have done. For all we know the questers could be alive and enjoying the challenges of that mysterious place. After all, danger is what adventuring is all about. All expeditions expect to meet hardships to be over-come along the way. Our magpie worries that his son has yet to fly home with news of the journey. Perhaps that chick-scout is too fired-up with excitement to think about us fretting here back home. As for Sedge's concern for his daughter Sage, I can only say "Like father, like daughter". As a chip off the old block, only a fool would risk her wrath if her friends were in danger. So be brave and hopeful, my family. All will come right in the end I'm sure. And now to the question of our pilgrim visitors. As we know they've come to worship the Great Snake who they hold as sacred, and to offer him a small gift in homage. Can we deny them their moment of joy just because we feel low on this beautiful morning?'

'The Pilgrims shimmer in their silver robes, Robin,' murmured Sedge. 'But are their hearts and thoughts as pure as their appearance? I urge caution.'

'And what do you think, magpie?' asked Robin.

'All that glitters is not gold,' mourned the bird. 'The treasure in my nest has turned to dross. I yearn for the return of two beady black eyes, for that's where true beauty lies.'

'Not very helpful at all,' frowned Robin. He turned to his soulmate, Fern. 'What do you think we should do?'

'We can only carry on to the end of our tale,' Fern sighed. 'Just as we pray that our questers are plodding on to their end of their different tail. I think we should help the pretty pilgrims who've travelled so far, guided only by the tail of a comet star. I'll add only one thing, Robin.'

'And that is?' he asked.

'That we heed the advice of wise old Sedge and be cautious. It's well known that our water vole friend has special bones that sense if something is right or wrong when they twinge him.'

'My twitching bones are undecided at the moment,' said Sedge. 'Perhaps we should give the Pilgrims the benefit of the doubt. While watching them closely, of course. Enemies come in many guises as we've learned to know, Robin.'

'So, a cautious benefit of the doubt it is,' said Robin. He turned to sweetly-smiling Brother Pilgrim. 'Today you and your friends will rest from your ordeal in our home tree. Then tomorrow we'll guide you up the buttercup hill and down into the cave where the snake's head lies trapped by the rocks he's long outgrown. Though we Willow folk are unhappy about our missing youngsters, that's no reason for you Pilgrims to be unhappy too. Your own long quest is almost at an end, Brother Pilgrim.'

'Thank you, Willow people,' said Brother

Pilgrim bowing low again. 'I just hope that our visit and gift will help to relieve the Great Snake's misery. Perhaps it might help him sleep awhile.'

'The great snake yearns for sleep above all things,' Robin nodded. 'If your worship and your gift could help him just to doze, that would be helpful. Though for deep and real slumber he needs the end of his lost tail to curl up with.'

'The tail in question being the one Robin and I intend to track down,' said Fern, determinedly. 'Setting off in the opposite direction to Finn and his team who I know are still alive and enjoying their adventure in The Wilderness. I just know it . . .' and she broke down and began to sob. Robin put a comforting arm around her.

'Our whole Willow clan is feeling the strain, you'll understand,' he explained to the faintly smiling Brother Pilgrim.

'Perhaps our visit and our gift can settle many problems,' he said gently. 'We have come with love and gift enough to ease all pain and worry. You sense our love, so why not taste the gift?'

'What a kind suggestion,' said Fern, wiping away her tears. 'I've never tasted the fabled honey from the nest of the bees who dream.'

'Perhaps a fingerful now, and for Robin too?' tempted Brother Pilgrim, turning and crooking a finger at the tiny chest-carrier.

'No, new friend,' said Robin, grandly. 'Our pleasures will wait. In the meantime I insist that you and your followers enjoy a long rest in our Willow clan home. Then after you have rested I intend to take you down into our dining-hall to enjoy a bowl of Granny Willow's famous stew.'

'Include me out,' muttered the little gift-carrier, his gold wig slipping sideways as sweat ran down his brow. 'I braved the famous spit of an orange toad and only just escaped with my life. I'm nil by mouth as far as anything famous is concerned.'

'My bones are starting to twitch, Robin,' said worried Sedge. 'And they seem to be warning us to be careful in the times ahead.'

But Robin and Fern were not listening. They

were already ushering the beautiful visitors up into their oak-tree home, determined to offer them every hospitality and the best of fare.

'My bones don't lie, magpie,' sighed Sedge. 'And they tell me they aren't in a trusting mood today. I have a notion about the visitors, and it worries me.'

'And I have a void in my heart,' croaked the sad bird. 'An emptiness that all the treasure in the lands of the People could not fill. I yearn to feel the rush of wings, and to gaze into the beady eyes of my wayward chick.'

'And I miss my daughter,' grieved Sedge. 'We can only pray that their adventure is treating them kindly, and that everyone comes home safe and sound.'

'I can only echo your words, old friend,' said the magpie, flapping away to his untidy nest to explain why their chick was still missing. Meanwhile Sedge swam slowly back across the stream to break similar news to his anxious family.

While Robin and Fern and their friends were entertaining their Pilgrim guests an old lady in her small kitchen was toiling with pots and pans and steaming ladles to create another of her sublime stews. As she measured and stirred and tasted large tears rolled down her cheeks and into her giant cauldron. Granny Willow was privately mourning the loss of tiny Nettles. She had been hurt for a while that his dream had been to become a great warrior instead of a great cook. She had accepted that. For when her own children had grown away from her, Nettles had become the love of her life. Among her pots and pans and amid clouds of steam, Granny Willow knelt and prayed for the safety of the boy who had come to mean so much to her.

Thirteen

A Reckoning in The Wilderness

While the bogus Pilgrims were being fêted and fed by the Willow clan, the questers were hurrying along the back of the snake in the wake of their forest guides. Though anxious to reach The Wilderness they were fearful too. From the tales the Forest folk had told them the place sounded like some kind of hell. But whatever awaited them there, nothing would make the questers turn back. For in that hell were two of their friends being held for ransom by the Scavengers. Though they had no treasure to bargain with they came bearing a rich anger that flashed and sparkled as bright as any diamond. But on reaching the edge of the forest it was hard to hide their dismay. As they gazed out at The Wilderness a scene of total desolation met their eyes. Never before had they looked on a landscape of such grim foreboding.

'It looks like the end of the world but hopefully isn't,' said Scarlet, gently tugging Finn's sleeve. 'Beyond The Wilderness must lie happier lands where the Great Snake winds beneath bluer skies.'

'Lands I'll never see, never explore,' said Finn bitterly. 'And nor do I deserve to. I'm thinking of the loyal warriors who died for my ambitious dream to lead a quest to the end of the Great Snake's tail. Now two more of our companions are facing death, waiting for us to rescue them. I speak of Sage and Nettles and should weep to speak their names. Once again I've failed as an explorer and leader. The questers bravely followed me and I must bear all guilt.'

'They followed because they believed in you, Finn,' said Scarlet softly. 'And they'll believe in you still if you believe in yourself. Now my friends and I must return to our forest home. Our weakness is we fear to dare, your strength is that you do.'

Finn agonised over her words as he gazed out on The Wilderness. There was no greenery there, not a note of birdsong that had kept their spirits high for so long. As far as the eye could see was flat, misty swamp. While here at the edge of the forest the sun dappled through the leaves, out there just nothing shone. Everywhere was wreathed in gloom and drifting mists. And there was the smell, the stench that came wafting in on a moaning wind, assailing the nostrils of the knot of questers standing forlornly on the back of the Great Golden Snake.

A vile smell of rotting vegetation and more awful things. Finn and his friends had noticed something else. While the back of the Great Snake had been dry and level through the forest, here the huge body plunged downwards to become almost submerged and floating in the thick, black waters of the swamp. Finn was jolted from his reverie by a firm hand on his shoulder and a voice in his ear. It was Pansy, her tone a little mocking.

'It suits you, Finn,' she said, her fingers playing with something around his neck. 'But then you could always charm the birds from the trees.'

'What is it?' Finn asked, bewildered. Then he looked down to see the circlet of red berries that had adorned Scarlet's hair.

'Lovingly placed there with her own fair hands,' grinned Pansy.

'When was this?' asked Finn, still confused. 'Where has she gone?'

'She and her friends returned to the forest,' said Pansy. 'While you were staring at nothing and dreaming, they were drifting like wraiths back into the trees.'

'Back to their lovely village and safety,' said Foxglove nervously. Coltsfoot put his arm around her but he felt rather frightened himself. In fact their mood was shared by most of the questers, including the warriors in their band. Every eye was on Finn, waiting for him to speak, to make a decision.

Suddenly the decision was taken from his hands. A piping voice drifted up from the murky waters below. It was shouting, 'Ahoy there,' in a nautical fashion Finn recognised. It was inquisitive Meadowsweet who made the first move. She rushed to peer down the snake's slippery slope, quickly joined by Teasel. Then she turned, amazement on her face.

'Three men in a boat,' she gasped. 'Rocking in the smelly ooze below.'

'Wrong,' grinned Teasel, straightening. 'There are three men in three separate boats, which is completely different.'

'You know what I mean,' fumed Meadow-sweet.

'No I don't,' teased Teasel. 'I'm here to make sure that what you scribble in your Quest Diary is accurate. I refuse to allow sloppy descriptions.'

Then Coltsfoot and Foxglove made a dash to the edge of the snake, to gaze down.

'Who are you, three men in three separate boats?' called Coltsfoot.

'Tell us who you are first,' replied the piping voice. 'And explain why you're standing in sunshine on the back of our Great Snake. We know you aren't Scavengers because Scumm and his gang came splashing and cursing past our camp only last night.'

'Were they dragging two prisoners with them?' yelled Foxglove. 'In the shapes of a water vole and a tiny boy with a cooking-pot?'

'We're not answering that,' said the piping voice stubbornly. 'Not until you've told us who you are. First things first, we say.'

'Why should we answer first?' retorted Foxglove. 'Tell us who you are and then we'll tell you who we are.'

'But if you lie to us, we'll lie back,' warned Coltsfoot.

'And we'll keep shouting lies at each other until we arrive at the truth,' Foxglove yelled. 'Which could take ages.'

'Be quiet and stand aside, I'll handle this,' said Finn, firmly in control again. He leaned from the top of the snake and peered down into the gloom. Teasel was right. There were three boats bobbing on the scummy waters, each containing a separate sailor. The boats were anchored to the golden scales of the near-submerged snake. But strangest of all, the boats were nothing more than large lily-pads. Even so they easily dwarfed the three green-clad sailors sitting inside them. Meanwhile the boatmen were staring fearfully up at Finn who was gazing curiously down. Then Finn found his voice at last. Smiling down, he seemed his old confident self again.

'What port do you hail from, jolly sailors?' he called jovially. 'I was once a sea-rover myself until the tide turned against me.'

'Saying you once sailed the seas isn't saying who you are,' said the tar with the piping voice suspiciously. 'Give us your precise name and bearings. Otherwise we'll cast off and find another berth in a quieter harbour.'

'And don't call us "jolly",' cried another sailor. 'There's nothing to be jolly about in The Wilderness where the sun never shines. Come clean with your names or we'll paddle away.'

'In that case, my name is Finn of the Fisher clan,' the proud leader replied. 'And my friends and I are bound on a quest to find the end of the tail of the Great Golden Snake, and to hurry it home to its grieving head. Now tell me who you are. Do you boat around for pleasure, or for purpose?'

'Boating for pleasure?' cried the piping voice, enraged. 'We are the Guardians of the Great Snake as he wallows and winds through The

Wilderness. Who do you think scrapes the barnacles from his belly, scrubs the weed from his flanks, and chases away the cheeky crabs who make homes in his scales? As for my name, as you've boasted about yours I'll boast about mine. I'm Misty, leader of The Wilderness Guardians, and I'm not a carefree sailor but a boat-girl with huge responsibilities. Does that dent your ego, proud Finn of the Fisher clan?'

'Not at all, mistress Misty,' apologised Finn.

'I also have some anger to release,' shouted the second boat-man. 'Take back that "jolly" word you tagged us with. Do we look at all jolly?'

'You certainly don't,' admitted Finn. 'Forget I ever said it.'

'And if you're thinking,' said the sour, third boat-man, 'that all we do is mess and potter around in boats, then think again. We've never found the idle time to indulge in such things.'

'If the thought crossed my mind them I'm truly sorry,' said Finn humbly.

'Now all anger is spent,' said Misty, satisfied and smiling. 'And warm welcomes are in order, plus our roomy boats. For countless generations we've tended to the needs of the Great Snake through this swampy part of his progress through the lands of the People. Our histories foretold that one day a hero would arrive on a quest to unite our Great Snake's head with his lost tail. And here you are, and we bless you. And now we offer you and your friends the meagre hospitality of our bleak Wilderness. But come, don't stand there framed against the sun. Just bring a snatch of it with you, a mere sniff will do.'

'But how do we get down?' asked Finn, puzzled. 'We've run out of level snake and your world is a long way down.'

'Just jump on the Great Snake and slide down his back,' said Misty. 'We'll be standing by to haul you aboard before you drown.'

Foxglove and Coltsfoot needed no urging. Uttering wild whoops they leapt on to the slope of the snake and whizzed down to plunge into the green-slimed waters below. They were quickly followed by Meadowsweet who judged her slide in order to keep her journal dry, and Teasel who grinned all the breathless way down, both landing in the safe boat. Nervous Umber went next and was rescued, spluttering, from the waves. Waving aside their protests, Finn ordered Pansy and the warriors and the others to launch themselves down before him. As their leader he was determined to go last. And then, after much splashing and yelling, all of the questers were safely aboard the giant lily-pad boats. Now their fate was in the hands of the mysterious Misty and her fellow boatmen. Tired, soaked and smelly, the questers obeyed when Misty briskly ordered them to paddle with their hands to help the over-laden craft along. Skilfully she steered a course along the water-logged body of the snake. Often the convoy of boats became wreathed in banks of fog and nudged off-course by the moaning winds. It seemed not to worry Misty and her friends. Generations of practice had taught them just how to cope with the moods of nature. A paddler in Misty's boat, Finn was filled with admiration as he watched the girl's slim arms wrestling with the tiller. Her skill as a sea-farer put his own to shame. Pansy paddling beside him could only fume and look daggers as she watched Finn watching Misty with a silly smile on his face. Then, above the sound of paddling hands and the sighing of the wind, Misty spoke as if to put them at their ease.

'We know about your kidnapped friends,' she assured them. 'When the Scavengers came wading through the marshes last night we could see they had prisoners with them. I suppose they've demanded a huge ransom of gold and jewels for the safe return of your friends. Are you carrying any riches in your packs? Enough to buy your dear ones back?'

'We're carrying nothing but a few provisions,' said Finn. 'The Scavengers robbed us of our personal things back in the cavern. Now we have nothing but strong arms and a deep hatred for Scumm and his thugs when we catch up with them.'

'A night-raid on Scavenger Island must be launched,' said Misty, heaving the tiller over. 'All friends of the Great Snake are our friends too. We hate the Scavengers even more than you, having endured their evil ways for countless years. First you'll be fed and allowed to rest at our camp before we strike at our enemy under the cover of darkness. I just hope you can fight as bravely as you talk, Finn of the Fisher clan. Our mission tonight will call for steady nerves.'

'Excuse me, mistress Misty,' said angry Pansy. 'There's no question about Finn's bravery. He's proved it many times throughout our quest.'

'Now he must prove it to me,' smiled Misty, wiping the spray from her face. At that moment Finn noticed that her eyes were as green as the seaweed cloak she wore. The soaking hair she tossed from her face was black, contrasting sharply with the whiteness of her skin. The black and white of the image prompted a sudden stab of guilt in Finn. In the hurried slide down the snake he had completely forgotten their injured magpie scout. Alarmed, for a moment Finn thought the bird had been left behind. But no. Perched on the prow of the boat was the young magpie, his wing drooping pitifully, his beak partly open as he uttered soft caws of pain. Finn was thankful to see that Foxglove was gently tending him. Then, suddenly, through the gloom dim lights could be seen. Misty ordered the paddling to cease. Standing up in the lily-pad boat she cupped her hands and called.

'It's we, the snake-cleaning convoy returning.'

'In time for a welcoming banquet,' drifted back the joyful reply.

'We return with friends from the lands of the sun,' called Misty again.

'In that delightful case we'll toss more shell-fish in the pot,' came back the answer. 'As welcome guests, we'll feed them till their bellies groan.'

Moments later the three boats were coasting into a small port, hedged on three sides by reed-huts raised on stilts. People began to flock to the shore, to watch the boats come in. Despite the dreary awfulness of The Wilderness, Misty's Guardian folk looked quite cheerful as they hurried to help the questers ashore. With their bright green clothes and their green eyes and their ready smiles, it was difficult to imagine that they had never seen the sun or heard a sweet bird sing. But it seemed that they had long ago accepted their lot and had risen above it to wrest some happiness from the misery around them. To make do, to make the best of life, that was the attitude of the folk who lived in the stilted camp. But then they were the carers of the Great Golden Snake in this part of the land. They were also of the People and fiercely proud of it. Once in the meeting hut the questers were plied with bowls of steaming fishy fare and heaps of tender greens that Finn detected as weeds and moss prepared in a delicious way. Sure enough, after two large helpings each of the bellies of the questers were groaning with overload. After answering streams of questions about the world outside, Finn and his weary friends were allowed to rest.

It seemed mere moments before Misty and some tough-looking Guardians were shaking them awake.

'Come, get up,' said Misty, urgently tugging Finn's arm. 'The night is here, and black as it will get. The rescuing raid on Scavenger Island is about to take place. Bring only your armed warriors down to the boats. Ours will be a fighting party when we steal ashore to surprise the Scavengers. The rest of your people will only get in the way if it comes to a battle.'

'That leaves me out then,' said Umber sadly. 'I

wish I was a warrior but I've always lacked the skills. My servile upbringing, you see.'

'Well my upbringing wasn't servile,' said Pansy angrily. 'So I'm going on the raid as well. And if anyone dares to point out that I'm a girl, then I'll snap back that so is mistress Misty.'

'But I'm also the leader of my Guardian family,' said Misty loftily.

'And I'm Finn's deputy leader,' retorted Pansy. 'And I can fight with the best of any warriors as you'll see.'

'She can,' admitted Finn, as Misty turned her green-eyed gaze on him.

'Very well,' said Misty briskly. 'Just her, but no more.'

There was no fear of any youngsters tagging along on the raid. They were all curled up fast asleep on their beds of soft reeds. Indeed the whole of the stilted camp was asleep save for the alert and gathering raiding party.

All except for one very sad soul. As the raiders stole by his hide in a thicket he spoke:

'Good luck Finn, good luck to you all,' said the magpie softly, his wing drooping and quite useless. 'The pain in my heart equals the pain in my wing. Now I'm just a burden to our quest which went so badly wrong during the fight with the Black Spiders. I should have flown back to the valley to raise the alarm. I could have brought Robin and Fern hurrying to the rescue, but I didn't. Instead I stupidly chose to join in the battle against the spiders and got my wings burned for it. Now here we are in this dreadful Wilderness, and here I squat, of no use to anyone. My father will be deeply ashamed when he learns that his son died of a broken heart and a singed wing in a lonely thicket, scorned and abandoned for letting his comrades down.'

'You've let nobody down, dear magpie,' soothed Pansy, peering into the thicket at the sad, beady eyes looking out at her. 'You're a hero to us, and you'll be a hero to your father when we finish this quest and return safely home. Just sit tight in that bush and rest as much as you can. We've got a small battle to fight, but we won't be long. Just keep your beak up, you poor down-hearted bird.'

'We haven't time for goodbyes,' hissed Misty impatiently. 'We're on a secret raid. Speed and silence are our vital weapons. Another girlish mistake from you and I'll order you back to camp. Is that clear, recruit Pansy?'

'Yes, mistress Misty,' said Pansy quietly. 'That was my one and only goodbye.'

'To the boats then,' whispered Misty. 'Remember, we paddle as softly as possible. The moon and the stars don't shine here in The Wilderness so the Scavenger guards rely on their ears to alert them to danger.'

Finn and his friends were still confused by the lack of light in the sullen Wilderness. Their eyes saw only black and varying shades of grey in this strange world. Yet Misty and her band seemed not at all bothered. Perhaps, over the long stretch of time they had lived in The Wilderness, grey was a coat of many colours to their adjusted eyes.

Once in the boats the raiders took up their paddles. Captained by Misty from the bow of her lead boat, the party silently paddled towards a hummock of blackness that suddenly loomed out from the grey surrounds. It was their destination, Scavenger Island, the home of the evil Scavenger clan. Silently they drifted into shore. Not so much an island, the hummock was a rare dry spot amid the ooze of the marshes. It was a shuddersome place to Finn and his friends as they climbed from the boats to follow Misty and her well-armed band up the squelchy beach to firmer ground. Excitedly, Misty nudged and pointed. Through the darkness could be seen a scattering of flickering lights.

'The hovels of the Scavenger clan,' whispered Misty. 'Somewhere down there are your captured friends. Let's hope they haven't been slaughtered, roasted and eaten. But probably not. Scumm will keep them alive in the hope that you'll come with a ransom of treasure. Then when he's got his greedy hands on that he'll set about to kill you all, that's how the Scavengers conduct their wicked business. But come . . .'

Gripping their weapons and ready for anything, the raiders crawled closer. Now the lights could be seen to be small fires. Edging nearer still they could make out small groups of Scavengers laughing and joking around the fires, turning disagreeable hanks of roasting things on spits. Away from the fires huddled a cluster of drab dwellings from which could be heard the crying of babies and the soothing songs of anxious mothers. A short distance away from those scenes burned a fire much brighter than the others. The raiders stalking even closer were horrified by what they saw. It was a blazing, smouldering midden-heap, the flames licking hungrily at the piles of rubbish the Scavengers had thrown from their hovels. But shockingly, amid the mounds of filth could be seen the feebly moving bodies of Sage and tiny Nettles. They were bound to stakes and seemed to be mouthing words to each other. Doubtlessly words of courage as death approached, surely last words of comfort for each other as their end neared. For Sage and tiny Nettles had lived as heroes, now they would die as such. It was a piteous sight to witness, prompting the furious raiders to spring into action. Seconds later they were on their feet and racing towards the flaming dump. At that same time Scumm was gorging down burnt flesh and laughing between swallows of strong, swamp ale. He was certain that soon his bitter enemy Finn would turn up with a huge amount of gold and jewels, to barter for the lives of Sage and Nettles. So he was happy and in a raucous mood as he addressed his comrades in crime around the fire.

'While we feast and await the riches the questers will bring, we'll sing of the lows in our lives, to remind us of harsher days. Who will sing our down-hearted song?'

'I will, Scumm,' said a bright-eyed, cowled

rascal, eager to please his master. 'I'm glad to sing of hard times past with the future so richly before us,' and he sang the down-hearted song to the delight of the Scavenger gang who would soon be rich beyond compare . . . or so they thought.

'Let us take heart
And not dismay,
We only lose
To fight another day.'

The Scavengers sitting around the fire looked suitably sad. They hated to be failed thieves and murderers. But yet they grinned. Quite soon the poverty of the past would be behind them, and they would stroll around the lands of the People like the lords they yearned to be. Scumm confirmed their ambitions.

'Now I will sing my new uplifting song,' he said. 'Composed while I was deep in thought about our future prospects.'

'Such a song we've been waiting for all our lives,' cried a Scavenger. 'Uplift us, Scumm, for we're banking on the ransom our prisoners will fetch.'

Scumm threw back his cowl to reveal the livid scar Finn had inflicted in the cavern. His bony face was a portrait of hatred as he began to chant:

'Let us rejoice
And shout hurray,
This time we'll win
And kill our enemy Finn,
To reap our treasure day.'

The Scavengers enjoyed the uplifting song much more than the down-hearted one. They sang it over and over again, quite unaware that the secret raiders were taking advantage of their rowdiness to rush and free Sage and Nettles from the burning rubbish-dump. Misty was firmly in charge.

'Don't speak,' she snapped, clapping a hand

over the mouth of a very astonished Nettles. 'You're being rescued by the Special Misty Squad. Just keep still while I slash your bonds with my dagger. Then I want you to run as fast as you can after me. There. But wait tiny boy, what's that you're hugging? We haven't the time to lug around mementoes of your captivity.'

'It's Granny Willow's cooking-pot,' said Nettles fearfully. 'I wouldn't dare run anywhere without it.'

'Just make sure it doesn't clank,' ordered Misty. 'This is a battle zone and the slightest noise could give us away to the enemy.'

'This empty vessel won't make a sound,' promised Nettles, scrambling to his feet. 'And please don't forget to rescue Sage, my best friend in the world.'

'That's being attended to,' said Misty briskly. She turned on a well-shaped heel. 'Now follow me down to the boats, small Nettles, and don't lose touch in the darkness.'

A similar event was taking place just paces away. The cruelly tethered water vole was rapidly freed and ushered down to the beach.

At that moment Scumm rose from the fireside. Ever suspicious, he wanted to check that his valuable prisoners still lay trussed on the rubbish-dump. For they were his passport to riches and thus precious to him. He smiled evilly as he walked alone, as alone as he always had been in spite of his fawning gang he secretly despised. His smile was for the tricks he still had up his sleeve. He knew the hated Finn would come to save his beloved ones from their fates worse then death. Scumm was sure that Finn would arrive with a huge ransom in exchange for their lives. But Finn was in for a great shock. Once the gold and jewels were in Scumm's hands he would order his gang to kill every last one of the questers. Then while that orgy was taking place Scumm would be slipping away from The Wilderness to a more pleasant land to live the rich and solitary life he had always yearned for. As he drew near the pile of burning filth he pulled his grey cowl over his hideous face. For he hated strangers to gaze on his ravaged features, even strangers quite soon to die. On reaching the burning tip he stood stock-still, the smile fading to an ugly grimace. Then Scumm threw back his head and uttered a wail, a huge and anguished cry. His prisoners, the surety of his future wealth, were gone. Spinning around, he began to charge like a maddened beast along the trail of muddy footprints that led down to the beach. He arrived to see people scrambling aboard the boats. Scumm just stood, his chest heaving, watching as all his dreams seemed set to slip from his greedy grasp. Again he bellowed his wrath and hatred as two of the lily-pad boats moved away across the still waters of the marsh. But one boat had not cast off. It was gently rocking in the shallows as if waiting. Then suddenly a solitary figure stepped from the grey shadows of a sandy dune.

'So here we are, face to face at last,' said Finn

quietly. 'I thought your greed would bring you here, foul Scumm. Well, your prisoners are rescued and on their way back to safety. As for the ransom you lusted for, it existed only in your twisted mind. Now, have we something to settle, you and I? I have a dagger, and so do you. Let the death of one of us close this argument.'

'I have no dagger,' protested Scumm, throwing back his cloak. 'I came here with no weapons at all. I've heard much about your honour, righteous Finn. Would you kill even your enemy while he was defenceless?'

'Now I have no weapons,' said Finn, throwing away his dagger and his sword and bow. 'My bare hands will do the job for me.'

'Why, just look what I have found,' sneered Scumm, drawing a thin, sharp blade from the top of his boot. Gripping it tight he lunged at Finn's startled face, screaming. 'First let me alter your pretty features as you did mine.'

Then suddenly he seemed to freeze, a look of amazement on his face. Still quivering in his chest was an arrow. He sank to the ground, pierced to the heart and dead.

'My claim on his life is greater than yours, Finn,' said Misty, shouldering her bow. 'He and his gang have terrorised my family for generations. Now the Scavengers are leaderless and won't recover for a long time. But you look surprised, Finn. Do you think that because I'm a girl, mine was a lucky shot?'

'I'm sure it wasn't,' replied Finn, still dazed from the speed of it all.

'So stir yourself,' ordered Misty, her green eyes twinkling. 'Gather your weapons and let's get down to the boat. They're waiting for us.'

All the way back to the little camp on stilts in the harbour of the Great Snake's body the rescued prisoners were fussed over. Sage, swimming alongside the boats was modesty itself as she was praised as a hero.

'I only did what I had to do,' she said, blowing shy bubbles as she swam along. 'Just as my father Sedge always did.'

In contrast, little Nettles was full of boasts. He was standing in the bow of the lead boat with his cooking-pot on his head.

'Of course,' he bragged. 'I never blurted a word. I endured all the tortures Scumm put me through, but I kept my mouth tight shut.'

'What were the secrets you wouldn't reveal?' asked Pansy, grinning but puzzled.

'Granny Willow's secret stew ingredients, of course,' said Nettles impatiently. 'Scumm and his gang only tortured with pain, but Granny Willow tortures with nagging which is much worse . . .'

And so, amid lots of relieved laughter and joy, the boats drifted in to their safe moorings. That night when most of the camp was asleep, Finn and Pansy and Misty and her friends talked long through the dark and starless hours.

'And will you go on?' asked Misty. 'Will you still travel on to find the end of our Great Snake's tail after all you've been through?'

'I won't force the questers to go on,' answered

Finn. 'They can turn back with my love and blessing. But I'll never give up my journey until I've gazed on the tail of the Great Golden Snake. For personal reasons I must prevail, I cannot fail.'

'Though darkness and misery all the way,' nodded Pansy loyally. 'I'll always be at the side of Finn.'

'With not a star to guide the way,' murmured Coltsfoot, sleepily half-listening.

'Nor moon and sun to light us through the dismal times,' yawned Foxglove. 'But we're going because, because . . .'

'The Great Snake's tail is there,' sighed Coltsfoot. 'And there's an end to it.'

'How far does The Wilderness extend?' asked Finn. 'We found our way in, there must be a way out.'

'The Wilderness stretches as far as our minds can reach!' said Misty, shivering. 'But we of this clan don't think of such things.'

'Tomorrow I set off along the Great Snake

again,' said Finn, determinedly. 'Alone or in company I won't turn back.'

'And neither will I,' said Pansy, her mind made up some time ago. If Finn went on, so would she. It was as simple and loyal as that.

Then everyone fell asleep beneath the brooding grey skies of The Wilderness, the only light, the colour of dreams . . . hopefully sweet for them all. Perhaps driven Finn was at last gazing at the end of the tail in his dream. So near and yet so far. But why not even nearer when he woke? Didn't dreams sometimes come true?

Fourteen

THE CRACK OF DOOM

The sun was just rising as the procession wound its way up the hill and on to the field of buttercups. Robin and Fern led the way. Alongside them limped Sedge, his bones still twitching, his mind still suspicious. Behind them walked Brother Pilgrim and his followers, their little gift-bearer puffing and panting from the weight of the chest he carried. The pilgrims were softly chanting a song, the words of which were hard to catch. Probably a song in praise of the Great Snake, thought Robin and Fern. Wise old Sedge was not so sure. As he limped alongside he urged his friends to be cautious, trying to explain what he still felt in his bones.

'Oh Sedge,' sighed Fern with a smile. 'Where is the harm in these beautiful pilgrims, so shy and gentle in their worshipping ways?'

'You're getting suspicious in your old age, Sedge,' joked Robin. 'But we honour your opinions so we will take care. Though I don't see how these nice people could possibly be a danger to us.'

As the procession began to push a path through the thick buttercup stalks the old magpie came flying in. Having been up and thinking most of the night he had made up his mind.

'Robin,' he said, hovering overhead. 'As I'm not needed here I'm off on a scouting trip, like in the old days. The pilgrims say that they passed our questers like ships in the night in The Wilderness. Well, I intend to take a look for myself. If our loved ones are still alive to be found, then I'll spy them out. For myself I can't believe they're dead, Robin. I don't have the bones of Sedge but my faith is as strong as his pains.'

'Fly safe, and I'm sure you'll find them wearied, yet joking about their hardships,' said Fern, prayerfully. 'And don't hesitate to scold them and order them back home. Tell them that they haven't failed but are just unsuccessful. Guide them home to our valley, dear magpie, for everyone misses them so.'

'Back home with a flea in their ear, every one,' promised the bird. 'And a flea in both ears for my thoughtless son, too lazy to fly home just once . . .' and off he flew high into the sky, his keen eyes mapping a course along the twisting coils of the Great Golden Snake. Then, on an impulse, he climbed even higher in the clear blue sky. What he saw made him curse his own stupidity. How many problems could have been avoided if he had taken this scouting trip a long time ago? For, hovering at a dizzy height, he could plainly see the whole of the snake's progress spread out below. Its huge body had described a near-circle around the lands of the People after its centuries of wandering. From his bird's-eye view the magpie was astonished to see that the tail of the snake was almost back home to the cave of tears where its head wept. The bird swooped down for a close look at a strange black wood, a mere stroll away from the valley of the Willow clan and the cave of tears. Perching in a tree he could see the bright golden tail of the great snake. It was pinioned to the ground by a thousand strong thongs, its constant struggling to no avail. Small figures hurried to and fro repairing the fraying bonds that held their captive down. Watching the cruel scene, the magpie began to understand the hatred and the fear the Doomsday clan felt for the Great Golden Snake. They had spent the whole of their existence striving to prevent the closing of the circle that they believed would spell the end of their world and their clan forever. Too saddened to linger, the bird soared back into the clear blue sky again. Soon he was back on course, gliding over the meadowlands and the green canopy of the Forest people and into the sunless mists and swamps of The Wilderness. He flew with an urgency and the power of the young magpie he had once been. He was the bearer of great news to the questers whom he prayed still lived. Yet bad news too. For they had been travelling in the wrong direction to reach the end of the tail. The wise words of Robin had been justified. That the end of the tail was probably much closer to home than one thought. But when, mused the bird, did the young ever pay attention to the words of their elders? And now he was lost in the bewildering world where the sun never shone. Swooping beneath the swirling mists of this awful place his anxious gaze scanned the dreary landscape that seemed to stretch forever around the bulk of the waterlogged snake. And then he saw the small encampment of huts raised on stilts above the marshes. Flying lower he began to make out small figures hurrying to and fro between a muddy beach and the camp. Lower and closer still, his heart leapt with joy. He could now clearly see the questers and delightedly his son perched nearby. Then the magpie was worried to notice that his son was trailing a wing and looking very sorry for himself. He dived down to investigate.

Meanwhile Robin and Fern and the pilgrims were shinning down the grass-woven rope and into the cave below. The Guardians instantly stopped their tending of the snake and stared nervously at the beautiful strangers suddenly in their midst. Robin hastened to introduce them to Amber who had taken charge in the absence of Umber. She was not impressed.

'Troubles piling on troubles,' she sighed. 'Aren't we busy enough? First you Willow people drop in with your plans to find and free the end of the snake's tail. And what did that dream come to, Robin?'

'We haven't heard from the expedition,' admitted Robin sadly. 'According to these kind pilgrims the questers are lost in The Wilderness.'

'Though hopefully still alive,' said Fern quickly. 'The magpie has gone to look for them.'

'And then we had the return of the comet,' said Amber, vexed. 'Some event that was. No sooner had it come streaking in when it was streaking out again with not a word of advice for our sleepless, weeping snake.'

'That wasn't our fault, Amber,' said Robin, annoyed. 'We don't control the heavens above.'

'We thought you did,' said Fern waspishly. 'With your star-gazing and your drum.'

'I'll let that nasty remark go,' said Amber. 'But what I won't let go is the way you clamber down into our cave of tears bringing strangers. Pretty strangers I'll admit, but strangers none the less.'

'If I could explain, lovely Amber,' said Brother Pilgrim, smoothly. 'My followers and I have travelled from afar, guided by that comet star to fall down in worship before the nose of the Great Golden Snake.'

'And we've come bearing a rare gift,' piped the small chest-carrier, setting down his burden and wiping the sweat from his brow. 'Gathered at life-threatening expense by yours truly.'

'We know that the Great Snake has a love of honey,' continued Brother Pilgrim. 'But has he ever tasted a comb of honey from a nest of the dreaming bees?'

'But that's the food of the Gods,' cried the Guardians, astonished. 'So rare that it doesn't exist except in dreams.'

'Many dreams are about to come true,' said Brother Pilgrim softly. 'And now if we may we'd like to pray at the nose of the Great Golden Snake.'

'And I will offer to the tip of his tongue the honey his taste-buds yearn for,' said the tiny pilgrim, quoting the words he'd been coached to say. And with great ceremony he opened the chest he had carried so far and placed it beneath the twitching nose of the weeping snake. As Robin and Fern stood respectfully aside, the pilgrims sank to their knees in the cave of tears. The Great Snake had opened his huge eyes and was gazing down into the opened chest his keen senses sniffing the contents. The aroma from the rare honey was of a perfumed sweetness. Yet he detected a strange bitterness too. An alarm rang in the Great Snake's brain. He shouted a warning but it was too late. The tempting honey was already being tested. Some of his faithful Guardians had scooped up fingerfuls of the delicious nectar and were gulping it down. Then watched by their astonished friends they began to sigh and drop stone-dead into the pool of tears. It was then that Brother Pilgrim knew he and his followers were unmasked. Now he took on his true self of Lord Stroller of the Doomsday clan, snarling his hatred and frustration as he looked wildly around for a means of escape. He dashed for the grass-rope still dangling down from the buttercup patch above. Angry Robin struck him full in his false face and yanked the rope free from its knot at the top. Now Stroller and his desperate followers began to mill around in search of another way out from their entrapment. Their search was fruitless. For the first time in his life Stroller no longer had the upper hand. He was defeated and he knew it. He crouched sullenly in a corner of the cave his former merciless arrogance gone, a cruel soul stripped bare to nothing. His followers began to wail to see their once-feared leader crumble so. Now they were leaderless and dreadfully afraid.

'Can't we fight, Lord Stroller?' cried the little bearer of the poisoned honey. 'Where is my hero of yesterday?'

'Crouched in a corner and dreading his wicked end,' shouted Amber, pointing.

Then the Great Snake began to speak. He was no longer the sad and weeping creature he had always been. For the first time in one thousand years he was thinking of others instead of himself.

'My children,' he cried, his voice cracking with anger. 'We know these pilgrims now as the Doomsday clan who've long sworn to kill me. Now they've murdered my friends and for that they must pay. Always they've believed that one day I would bring their world to an end. Then so shall it be. Strength floods through me with a terrible rage. Now my enemies and the murderers of my friends will suffer the ending of their world as their histories foretold.'

'But what of us, your faithful Guardians, Great Snake?' cried Amber in fear. 'Take vengeance on your enemies if you will, but this is the only home we've ever known. What shall we do? Where shall we go? We need your guidance at this terrible time.'

'The secret passageway that leads to the stars, Amber,' urged the snake. 'Take it. Hurry your family and friends away from this cave of tears.

Take refuge among the kindly Willow people and build your lives anew in the sun. Go quickly now, and my blessings on you all. Seal the way to the world above behind you when you flee. For I have a date with Destiny to keep, and my long patience is running out . . .'

Needing no further urging, Amber yelled for everyone to follow her. Every Guardian plus Robin and Fern were hard on her heels as she dashed for her secret exit hewn through the rock of the cave. There was one other escaper as nimble as anyone. The small lookout cum chest-bearer of the Doomsday clan was as eager as anyone to escape from the cave. He had never thought much of Lord Stroller and the histories of the Doomsday clan that had been drummed into him from a child. He had always secretly believed that to live and let live was the road to happiness. For a moment his hopes dropped as Fern made to stop him entering the secret passageway. But a glance in his pleading eyes changed her mind and she tumbled him inside.

Once inside the tunnel everyone took their cue from Amber who began to claw at the loose rocks of the roof and the walls. Soon lots of hands were willingly joining in. There was a rumble and a huge cloud of dust as the tunnel collapsed, sealing the cave of tears from the world above. Then everyone was hurrying along the choking tunnel to reach fresh air and the glorious sunshine above. But there was no time to bask in the beauty of the day as they raced as fast and as far away as possible from the calamity they knew was about to take place. Sedge, ever present, ever kind, gladly bore the weaker ones to safety on his broad back despite his aching bones. Down the hill they tumbled, gasping and stumbling in their frantic flight. The soft green grass of the valley below was bliss beneath their toes as they ran the last breathless lap towards the safety of the great oak of the Willow clan. Once there and exhausted they were grateful for the firm but gentle hands that lifted them from the ground and up into the security of the tree-home. There, from every vantage point throughout the oak the Guardians and Willow folk gazed towards the hill, their faces filled with fearful expectation. Something enormous was about to happen, they just knew. Something that could even change their lives forever. And much sooner than they thought . . .

Fifteen

LIGHT BREAKS WHERE NO SUN SHINES

There came a low rumbling noise like far-off
thunder. All at once the valley and the surrounding countryside began to tremble from waves of
shock. Leaves and branches torn from the trees
rained down on the terrified People as they
hugged each other for comfort among the stout
boughs of their ancient home. The stream, ever a

secure highway through their valley, began to foam as its old bed shifted to confuse the flowing waters. Suddenly the hill of the buttercups burst open with such fury as to send great boulders hurtling into the sky, the blue of day blackening as clouds of dust blocked out the sun. It was an earthquake to equal any recorded in the histories of the People down the ages. But the frightened and transfixed watchers knew that this was no natural event of nature. They knew that this was the awesome work of the Great Golden Snake goaded beyond endurance to put an end to his centuries of misery. A snake venting his rage on his Doomsday enemies and on the rocky tomb that had held him prisoner for so long. Then, as the rumbling and the crashing of huge boulders died away, an astonishing sight hazily appeared through the clearing clouds of dust. As the sun began to shine once more, the snake could be seen in all his enormous glory, newly burst and born again from the bowels of the earth. Freed from a lifetime of captivity, his golden nose rested on what remained of the hill, his green eyes glowing with joy, his flicking tongue tasting the fresh air for the very first time. Then another awesome event took place. The snake's body began to pulsate, sending powerful ripples along his golden skin. Gathering force and speed, the ripples swept through the now shattered cavern to the grassy knoll. Then onwards they sped through the meadowlands and the forest and into The Wilderness, never once pausing in that journey around the giant circle its body described. The great snake raised his head and turned his delighted gaze upon the oak in the valley and winked an enormous green eye. It was as if he was telling his friends to just wait for his next trick. It came quickly and as if by magic.

'Just look!' gasped Amber, needlessly pointing, for all could see for themselves.

'I always knew that the tail was nearer, rather than farther away,' murmured Robin to Fern who was clutching his arm.

'And I always knew you knew,' whispered

Fern as everyone gazed at the astonishing sight taking place before their eyes.

The black wood, a mere meadow and hill-stroll away from the head of the snake, had exploded, the force sending showers of uprooted trees flying into the air like matchwood. As this second eruption slowly settled so a bright golden glow began to squirm and slide across the short divide, growing larger and more magnificant as it approached. It could only be, it had to be . . .

'The tail of our Great Snake is finally coming home!' cried Amber, tears streaming down her face. 'And see how that beloved nose reaches to kiss his long-lost end, his reunited friend.'

'And not before time,' said her fellow Guardians, wet-eyed each one'. A returning tail looking exactly like our clever artists painted it from imagination. Even more handsome in fact.'

'We must rush back to share our dear friend's joy,' cried Amber excitedly. 'After all, the return of his tail was our desire too.'

'We'll all go back to buttercup hill,' grinned Robin. 'Or what's left of it. We Willow people are as glad as anyone that the Great Snake is whole again.'

'I'm glad that you're glad, Robin,' smiled Fern. 'It's such a long time since you've had something to be glad about.'

'Could I share the gladness too, Fern?' appealed the little poison-carrier, tugging at her tunic. 'I was always miserable being Lord Stroller's slave. He was always forcing me to do wicked things against my will.'

'With us you'll always have free will, little one,' promised Fern, giving him a hug. 'Now that Lord Stroller and his evil followers are dead, you can put your dreadful past behind you. From this day on you'll begin a new life as a free spirit among we Willow folk.'

'Thank you, kind Fern,' said the tiny poisoner humbly. 'Never again will I do bad things, but only good ones. Later I'd like to thank you in the only way I can. I know the secret nesting place of the dreaming bees. I'd like to bring back a delicious, dripping honeycomb for the Willow clan to enjoy, to express my own joy.'

'Perhaps some other time, small eager one,' said Fern hastily. 'When we get to know you better.'

Everyone in the great oak agreed that climbing up what was left of buttercup hill was a good idea. They all wanted to share in the happiness of the Great Golden Snake. Even Granny Willow put down her stew-ladle and joined the throng wending up the shattered hillside to marvel at the Great Snake and share his joy. Sedge had bravely rescued his frightened family from their flooded burrow across the stream. Now he limped up the hill beside Robin and Fern, his adoring brood close on his heels. It was a difficult climb through the debris of tumbled rock and ankle-deep dust but well worth it. The reward was to see the snake in all his glittering glory, his huge chin lovingly resting on the tip of his long-lost tail. It was a moving sight to see the pair of them so long apart, now so naturally close. Granny Willow wept when she saw the happy couple. She was thinking of her tiny, adopted Nettles lost in The Wilderness and feared for dead. And he could have become such a talented cook, she grieved. She was not alone in her weeping.

'To think we Guardians would live to see our snake in sunshine,' sobbed Amber. 'And our clan in sunshine too. If this is a dream then let it never end.'

'This is no dream, my precious one,' smiled the giant, flicking out his tongue to gently wipe away her tears. 'Thanks to the devotion of the People I regained my strength and broke free from the cave that imprisoned me. And did I destroy the world that the Doomsday clan so feared?'

'No, Great Snake!' shouted Amber. 'Our peaceful world is as safe as ever, and much the brighter for your presence upon it.'

'Yet the histories of the Doomsday clan did

indeed come true,' mused Robin. 'You did destroy a world. Their own wicked one.'

'I hope the Great Snake doesn't spot me,' shuddered the little poisoner, hiding behind Fern. 'For I'm the last of the Doomsday clan and he might wipe me out root and branch.'

'Don't be silly,' chided Fern gently. 'The Great Snake is a kindly and forgiving soul. He'll understand that you've turned over a new leaf, and you are not the chill-eyed poisoner you once were.'

'What poison?' said the tiny one indignantly. 'I've never handled poison in my life. If I did it was a pure mistake.'

'There, you see,' soothed Fern.' Your turned-over leaf is beginning to work.'

Then the grateful snake began to speak again. His green eyes were filled with love as he gazed down and addressed the crush of tiny people below.

'Thanks to you, my friends, I'm whole again. Now I can curl up with my tail and sleep at last.

Or perhaps just nap for a year or two. For life is so wonderful now I'd hate to sleep away too much of it. And now it's my turn to do something unselfish for the first time in my life. What can I do to thank you for everything you've done for me? Make any wish, and if I can I'll grant it.'

'There's only one thing we wish,' said Robin sadly. 'Our happiness would be complete if our questers could come home safe to us. But alas, they're lost in The Wilderness, perhaps lying dead, killed by the Scavengers who roam that dreadful place. Now we have only a faint hope to cling to . . .'

'Make that a large hope,' cried the magpie, winging in from his long flight. He perched on a nearby rock to recover his breath. Then he grinned as he glanced around at the sad faces, at the snake glittering in the sunshine with his tail at last returned. He eyed the snake with a twinkly, beady look. 'Been having a bit of a spring-clean, I see. I wondered what all the noise and the clouds of dust were about. I could hear the din from miles away. I'm glad you finally stirred yourself to do something about your situation instead of weeping all the time. After hundreds of years of crying you must have bored countless generations of these faithful Guardians.'

'Excuse me, magpie,' interrupted Fern. 'Would you repeat your first words? Don't tease us as you usually do, just say them again.'

'After I said "only a faint hope to cling to",' prompted Robin.

'My words were, "make that hope a large one",' said the bird, grinning even wider. 'For I'm delighted to say that our questers are not lying dead in The Wilderness but are alive and kicking. Just a few minutes ago I left them moping about in a sea of mud looking very sorry for themselves. Finn was trying to rally them to continue the trek to the end of the tail, But looking at our Great Snake's cosy scene, their trip would be pointless, not to mention endless. If the truth is known our small ones are thoroughly miserable and would love to come home. Only pride is keeping them going, and it wasn't for me to interfere. When I left them my son was pretending his injured wing wasn't hurting a bit, but . . .' and a shocking thing happened. The bird so well known for masking his love and loyalty with teasing and jokes broke down, his wings drawn over his face to hide his tears.

'The questers will be rescued!' cried Robin as others began to weep. 'I intend to organise another expedition to bring them safe home.'

'And I'll be Robin's second-in-command,' vowed moist-eyed Fern.

'I'm going too,' said Amber determinedly. 'For my Umber is out there somewhere.'

'Perhaps I can help,' interrupted the Great Snake, his eyes glowing with excitement. He twitched the end of his enormous tail. 'Why trek into The Wilderness when you can glide there in comfort?'

Fern grasped his brilliant idea immediately. 'Of course, how clever of the snake. Now he has complete control of his tail he can order it anywhere he wants. If we climb aboard it we can travel to The Wilderness in style, Robin.'

'I'm worried about the hardship,' said Robin reluctantly. 'All worthy expeditions need a certain amount of hardship to make them remembered for all time.'

'Oh, come on,' said Fern impatiently. 'We're not worrying about the histories of our clans now, but for the lives of our young ones trapped in The Wilderness.'

She began to clamber up the golden scales of the waiting tail, the little Doomsday poisoner clinging desperately to the hem of her tunic. He had made up his mind she was going nowhere without him. He needed her kindness and protection while he tried to live down the evil roots from which he had sprung. While he himself believed he had changed from bad to good, others might believe he was still the tiny turncoat of his former days. So he was taking no chances. He was sticking to his saviour Fern like a leech.

Soon Robin and Amber had joined them on top of the tail of the snake. Others eager to travel were sternly ordered down again by Robin who had taken on the role of captain for the glide around the lands of the People.

'Good luck, and bring everyone safely home,' cried the crowd, clapping and cheering as the Great Snake rippled his muscles and ordered his tail to set off.

'How I'd love to go,' sighed Sedge. 'If it weren't for my aching bones I'd do so.'

'Me too, but for my weary wings,' agreed the bird regretfully.

'At least our youngsters will soon be in safe hands,' murmured the water vole. 'Robin and Fern will bring them home to us.'

'For our faith is strong,' agreed the bird.

'As the faith of the People has always been strong,' echoed the crowd as the tail slid away bearing its precious cargo of rescuers. As it slithered from view not one soul slipped away to attend to other business. Without fuss they would remain standing firmly beside the nose of the Great Golden Snake until their loved ones returned. If they had to wait forever, then so be it. For they were of the People and their thoughts were simple. But they possessed a mighty faith that soared above all clever words and reason.

Along its own neck slid the bright golden tail, the passengers clinging tightly to its scaly back. Now they were gliding through the cavern blasted and opened to the sky by the fury of the great snake. Soon they were cruising past the grassy knoll where the questers had once camped for the night. The journey through the meadowlands was like floating across a green sea of poppies and daisies and gently flitting butterflies. Ever beside was the hulk of the great snake's flank, its hanging growth twitching as thousands of snall creatures peered curiously out to watch the tail and its crew pass by. Then began the twisting passage through the forest. The noise of cheering was loud in the ears of the rescuers as Scarlet and Old Ashwold and all the People of the forest turned out on the back of the snake to wish the party good luck. The sudden plunge from dappled sunlight into darkness was shocking. Without a pause the tail slipped down into the murky waters of The Wilderness and floated determinedly on. The passengers gasped as the cold spray dashed over them, shuddered as the moaning winds chilled their bones. Standing at the very tip of the tail, Robin craned his eyes but could see only more hazy mist ahead. But wait . . . what were those pinpoints of light piercing the gloom dead ahead? The tail of the snake surged on . . .

Not too far away Finn and the questers were preparing to set off on the next lap of their journey to find the end of the tail. Everyone

311

was making an effort to appear determined and keen as they shouldered their packs in readiness for the march. In fact, only their loyalty to Finn was keeping them going. They had come to hate The Wilderness and longed to see the sun again. The thought of more dreary sameness stretching before them was a dismal prospect. What Finn himself thought he kept to himself, though his usual confidence seemed a little forced as he moved among his friends with a joke here, a word of advice there. So it was a great delight to everyone when the old magpie came soaring down through the mists to alight among them. He was welcomed with much gladness and pestered for news from home. As he answered their questions he was distressed to see the pitiful state of his son. It was then he implored them to give up their impossible journey and return home.

'I must warn you all,' he cried. 'From high above I've seen what lies before you. Just stark wilderness and swamps and mist for as far as my eye could see. I plead with you to give up and come home, brave youngsters. You've done your best, that's all anyone can do.'

'Would you give up, Dad?' asked his injured son.

'That question is unfair,' replied his father, tears in his eyes. 'But very well, go on if you must. And I must go back to our valley to break the news that you won't be coming home. It's news I'll bear with a heavy heart, though better than news of your deaths. Travel with my love, brave children. Just come back alive whatever the outcome of your stubborn quest . . .'

Moments after he had flapped away the questers were startled by a series of deep rumbling noises and violent tremors rippling along the body of the snake. The turgid waters lapping against his bulk began to slap and foam, shaking the flimsy stilt-legged homes of The Wilderness folk. After a worrisome while, however, all was still again.

'Something strange has happened,' said

Misty, nervous and puzzled. 'Our Great Snake has never reacted so violently to an earth tremor before. Something weird is going on and I don't know what!'

'Perhaps the end of the world has begun,' whispered Pansy. 'Perhaps the Doomsday clan were right in their beliefs. Perhaps in our absence the Great Snake has closed the circle with his tail and is beginning to crush the life from our lands.'

'Impossible,' said Finn firmly. 'I launched this quest to find the end of the tail. My explorer's instinct tells me that it's still out there somewhere. It could hardly have returned home while I'm still searching for it.'

'Why not?' asked Misty, her green eyes intent on him. 'What drives you, reckless Finn? What makes you trek on to the end of a tail that might not be there when you finally arrive to where you think it should be?'

'Because it's there,' replied stubborn Finn.

'Or perhaps your dream lies there,' said

Misty, her voice sad and gentle. 'Your dream to succeed for once in your life . . .'

Suddenly Umber was on his feet, shouting and pointing towards the bleak horizon. He rarely became excited so it had to be something important.

'Here comes the sun,' he gabbled. 'Brightening the darkness and advancing towards us. It has to be a good omen, Finn.'

'And getting closer and brighter every second,' gasped Meadowsweet, gazing, 'it's like one of my poems coming to life, full of lightness where no sun shines.'

'That isn't the sun,' said Teasel, bringing her down to earth. 'Bright it certainly is, but romantic it certainly isn't. As it comes closer it's beginning to look quite practical to my eye.'

'Teasel's right,' said Coltsfoot, peering. 'It can't be the sun skimming over the water towards us. I can see people standing on it and waving at us. According to my studies of the stars, suns are much too hot to stand on.'

'My sums are the same as Coltsfoot's,' said Foxglove, having a good peer herself. 'And what is more the wavers on the golden craft are beginning to look familiar. If I'm not mistaken it's Robin and Fern come to rescue us from this starless nightmare. I can only say, thank heaven for that.'

'And it looks like they're riding on the tip of our Great Snake's tail!' yelled joyful Umber. 'Where on earth did it come from . . . would you believe it?'

'All will be explained later,' yelled Robin as the tail wriggled in to berth smoothly upon the shore. 'Just scramble aboard and let's get out of this terrible place.'

Not one quester needed telling twice. At this moment they weren't in the least interested to know how the tail they had set out to find, had found them instead. To be honest the youngsters were weary of travelling around a giant circle that never seemed to end. Even Finn was relieved to be rescued, though he didn't show it. And he never would, his pride being so involved. He knew that great explorers never admitted defeat, only to suffering setbacks. The shocking arrival of the end of the tail would always be a setback in his mind. He tried to look very dignified as he climbed up the stepping-stone scales to the top of the golden tail. Amid the eager scrambling to get on board only Pansy noticed his sad eyes and slumped shoulders. She went to sit close beside him, offering a hug as the fully-laden tail began to slither off the beach.

'Take heart, Finn,' she whispered. 'Your first expedition to find the source of the River of Dreams ended in failure. Now this quest to find the end of the tail has also failed. But the failing isn't important, Finn, for your worth is in the striving. Which makes you a special failure. One day you'll put this time of shame behind you and go on to be a great explorer. I think it will be third time lucky for you, sad Finn. And on the day when you set off fully equipped to restore your shattered reputation I'll be beside you every step of the way.'

And then the glittering tail began to turn about for the long glide back to its head. As it began to forge through the swampy water a plaintive voice called out from the shore. It was Misty, her slim arms upraised, her hair a wild tangle as the sad winds moaned around her.

'We know The Wilderness is a God-forsaken place,' she cried. 'But it's our home. Don't ever judge us for how we live, but for what we are. The end of the tail has come home and we're glad for our Great Golden Snake. But when you get back remind him that we Guardians in The Wilderness will always tend and scrub his body to look nice and spruce every new morning.'

'And so will we, mistress Misty,' shouted Umber and Amber, waving to her as tears rolled down their pale cheeks. 'Though our great friend has found peace we'll tend him faithfully while he sleeps.'

*   *   *

'Here they come at last!' cried the joyful crowd around the snake's head. 'Wearied but rescued, that's the main thing. And not a culprit can we see among them. Every precious face glows with innocence, with not a trace of guilt. Welcome, our dearly beloved lost ones.'

The first to slide down from the tail of the Great Golden Snake were Robin and Fern. They were greeted with loud cheers. Then came Coltsfoot and Foxglove to applause just as loud. Umber and Amber were next. They were greeted with a reception that made them blush with pleasure. The moment wounded Sage and the limp-winged magpie appeared they were smothered with sympathy and patted a lot before being bustled away by their proud but concerned parents. The magpie chick and the water vole daughter had earned their spurs as worthy successors to a proud heritage. As Finn and Pansy clambered down they were greeted with claps and murmurs of deep respect. The watchers knew that they were just learners in the art of exploring. And though they had failed, at least they had tried and failed. Then Nettles came gambolling down, his cooking-pot helmet firmly on his head. While the others had showed modesty, Nettles began to strut up and down, his swagger causing some to tut and sigh.

'Who'll be presenting me with the medal for extreme bravery?' he cried. 'But for my presence the expedition would have foundered completely. I won't boast about how many enemies I slew with bow and sword, but it was a lot. And I can see that the Great Snake has found the end of his tail he so carelessly misplaced. I expect he'll wish to grovel and thank me for the large part I played in finding it.'

'You mean the end of the tail found you!' shouted a voice from the crowd amid much laughter.

'And I hope you've kept that cooking-pot sparkling clean,' scolded Granny Willow, waddling from the crush to take him by the ear. Nettles protested bitterly as she led him away.

'But Granny Willow,' he was heard to wail. 'I'm now a proven, first-class warrior.'

'Prove yourself a first-class cook then I might listen,' she was heard to reply. 'In the meantime there's a pile of dirty stew bowls in need of washing back in my spotlessly clean kitchen.'

Then the fluting voice of Meadowsweet was heard. She still wore the flowered hat she had set off in, though now it looked rather battered and worn. Under her arm was tucked her precious journal that contained the complete record of The Quest To The End Of The Tail, scribbled down in her crabbed and fussy hand. She made no attempt to scramble down from the tail of the snake as the others had. Instead she posed on the golden scales and waved regally to the chuckling crowd below. Then grandly she opened her journal and waited for silence. Behind her stood Teasel, grinning as widely as ever.

'My Willow clan people,' she began, her voice high and clear. 'In the days to come you will all be rushing to the library to read for yourselves the amazing adventures I've faithfully written down. But I'm sure you are desperate for a snatch from it right here and now. And so to whet your appetites, here it is in the form of a poem, written while sliding home on the tail beneath me.' And in bell-like tones she began to quote:

'We marched away the miles and miles
Attacked by Scumm and Stroller's guiles,
But led by Finn we braved our trials
With sturdy hearts and beaming smiles.'

There was a smattering of polite applause from the crowd. Then Teasel stepped forward.

'You will recognise that as a typical Meadowsweet poem,' he said, slyly. 'If by some chance you stampede to read her journal, you'll find it on the library shelf among the butterfly and pretty flowers books. On the other hand, if you want to read my darkly secret journal that I kept throughout the quest, look on the shelf entitled Tales of Dreadful Horror And Mystery, by the poet Teasel.'

'How dare you!' stormed Meadowsweet, stamping her blistered bare foot. 'I endured the same hardships as you on our quest, and I wrote about it truthfully. My journal will have a special place on the shelf that catches the light.'

'And remain there forever unread,' grinned Teasel. 'Except by me. For I've always had a soft spot for you, no matter what rubbish you write.'

'Pure jealousy,' snapped Meadowsweet. 'Well, there's one person who loves my poems and I'm going to read it again just for him.'

But she was wasting her time. The Great Golden Snake had fallen fast asleep for perhaps a brief year or two, the end of his long-lost tail tucked comfortably under his chin.

It was also time for the Willow clan and their friends to drift home for bed. It had been a long and extraordinary day. Indeed, some many long and anxious days. The sun had sunk below the hills as they arrived back at their oak tree home in the valley. The quest to find the end of the tail was over. So was their own personal tale, until another arose to challenge them.

In the wind-whispering galleries, through the snoring sleeping-quarters, in the hush of the sacred library drifted the spirit of the People, ever protecting while the gentle folk slept.

The tail of the snake had come full circle. So, too, had the tale of the People. With the sky blazing with stars and the moon riding over the trees, to make the night quite perfect a nightingale sang in a thicket in the valley . . . in the blessed lands of the People.

THE ARK OF THE PEOPLE

W.J. Corbett

THE FIRST STORY IN THE ARK OF THE PEOPLE SEQUENCE

In their ancient oak the miniature Willow People live in peace and harmony with nature. But humans flood the valley.

In a desperate bid to survive, the People set sail in an oak-bough Ark. Somewhere beyond the floods is a new life for them, a new home. They will need all their courage to find it.

But they have also saved Deadeye of the Nightshade Clan and his host of vicious allies. Now it is more than courage they will need . . .

Another Hodder Children's Book

THE SPELL TO SAVE THE GOLDEN SNAKE

W.J. Corbett

THE THIRD STORY IN THE ARK OF THE PEOPLE SEQUENCE

The Willow Clan of the People live peacefully with their neighbours, the Guardian Clan who tend the Great Golden Snake.

But others from afar have heard of a snake made of gold. Hell-bent on plunder, marauding warriors are heading towards the valley.

Again the youngsters of the Willow Clan take up the challenge. As they prepare to defend the valley, they turn to the wizard Berrybottom and his famous magic spells . . .